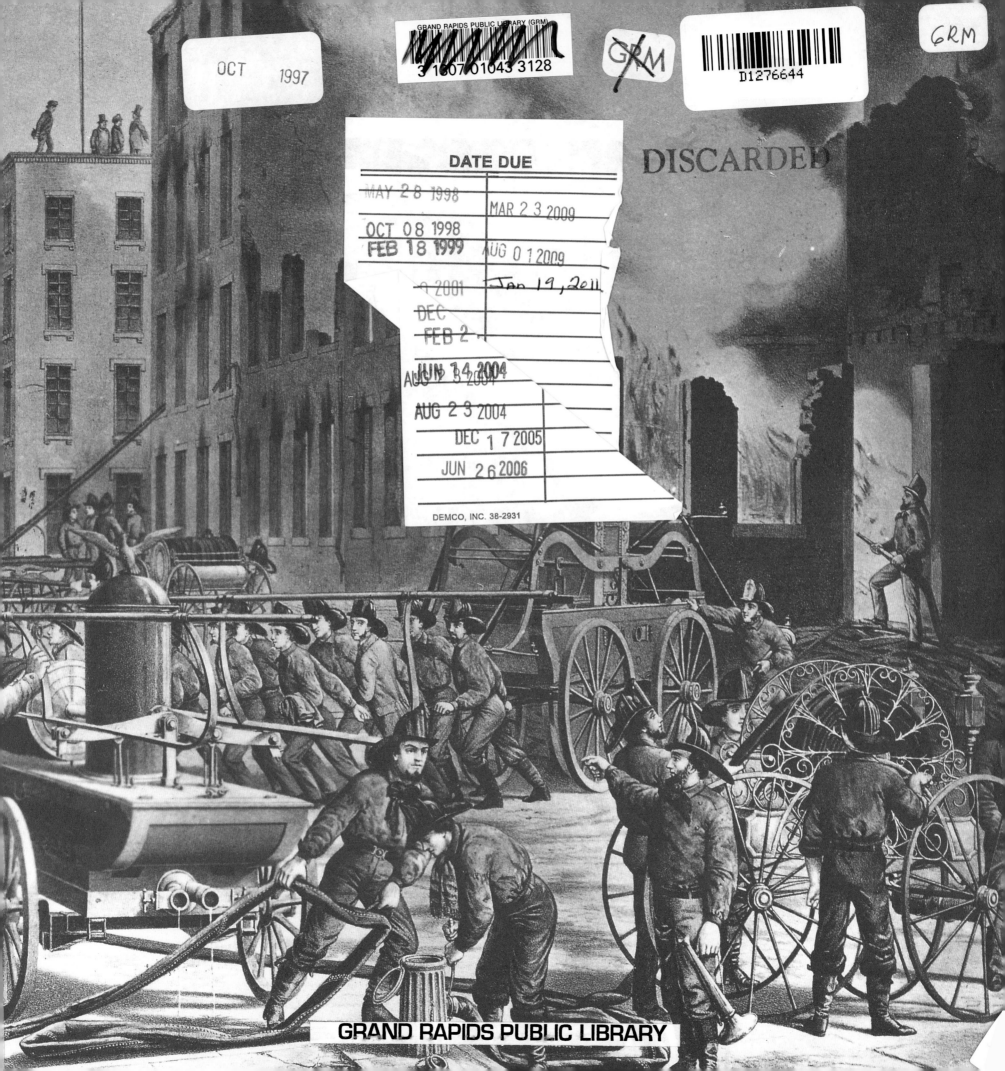

FIRE ENGINES

FIRE ENGINES

ROB LEICESTER WAGNER

MetroBooks

MetroBooks

An Imprint of Friedman/Fairfax Publishers

© 1996 by Michael Friedman Publishing Group, Inc.

Library of Congress Cataloging-in-Publication data available upon request.

ISBN 1-56799-382-6

Editor: Tony Burgess
Art Director: Lynne Yeamans
Designer: Galen Smith
Photography Director: Christopher C. Bain
Photography Editor: Emilya Naymark

Color separations by Ocean Graphic International Company Ltd.
Printed in China by Leefung Asco Printers Ltd.

For bulk purchases and special sales, please contact:
Friedman/Fairfax Publishers
Attention: Sales Department
15 West 26th Street
New York, NY 10010
212/685-6610 FAX 212/685-1307

Visit the Friedman/Fairfax Website:
http://www.webcom.com/friedman/

DEDICATION

Dedicated to my nephew, Cory Howard Macy, a future fire-fighter; and to my wife, Deniece Heredia-Wagner.

ACKNOWLEDGMENTS

Many people were involved in providing valuable assistance to me in writing this book. Without their contributions, the text would never have been written. I'm particularly grateful to Dr. Peter Molloy, director of the Hall of Flame Museum in Phoenix, Arizona.

I also want to thank the following California firefighters for their contributions: Garden Grove firefighter Allen Bone, codirector of the Pioneer Fire Company Museum in San Bernardino, and Bill Messersmith, volunteer firefighter for the Sierra Madre Fire Department.

The Riverside Fire Department was especially helpful in my research on specialized departments, such as hazardous materials. Special thanks to Public Information Officer Joan Breeding Letbetter, Firefighter Stan Futch, Battalion Chief Jerry Barden, and Captains Jerry Mungerson and Joe Rosales.

Bryan Deyo, captain of the San Jacinto Fire Department and staff member of the *Inland Empire Firefighter's Gazette*, also provided Haz-mat information.

Donald Baird, of Oakville, Ontario, Canada, provided information about Canadian fire-fighting history.

A debt of gratitude also goes to Alan Gilliam of Riverside, owner of a pristine 1944 Seagrave Pumper, who provided extensive information about Seagrave fire engines.

CONTENTS

INTRODUCTION

When I was a kid living in Sierra Madre, California, the air horn atop City Hall would blast at noon on the last Friday of each month as part of a civil defense test.

The neighborhood kids would stop what they were doing and ponder the likelihood of a nuclear attack for a moment before resuming play. We never actually believed that such a calamity would occur, but the continuing blasts from the horn still stopped us.

But when the horn sounded on days other than the last Friday of the month, that really caught our attention. It meant only one thing: there was a fire someplace, and the city's forty-four-man volunteer fire department was responding to the alarm. And if we happened to be nearby, it was quite a sight to see the firefighters racing to a blaze in their private cars, then jumping out still struggling to get into their turnouts, big rubber fire boots, and heavy coats. It was obvious to me even then—at the impressionable age of ten—that these guys really enjoyed responding to, and fighting, fires.

I once had the opportunity to summon the Sierra Madre Volunteer Fire Department myself when a small brushfire broke out at the rear of an old ramshackle wooden house less than a block from my home. Even at a young age I knew my duty was to call the fire department (these were the days before 911). The thrill wasn't so much in calling them, but in sitting on the curb knowing they would arrive on the scene in less than three minutes. And sure enough, they did.

The Sierra Madre Volunteer Fire Department was housed in a garage adjacent to the old City Hall, a Spanish adobe building with a red tile roof built in 1927, when everything in California was built out of adobe and topped off with a red tile roof.

Every year the fire department held its fire prevention safety program for children. We were allowed to climb over the department's pair of Crown pumpers and an old Seagrave, and wander through the second-floor meeting room that had been converted to storage. The slide pole, not used in many years, still remained shiny from the countless hands of firefighters long gone.

The old City Hall has since been converted to an office building, and in 1976, the fire department's digs were moved a couple of blocks down the street to a new building with much less personality but much more efficiency and comfort.

But Sierra Madre, with a population of around ten thousand, still has a volunteer fire department, typifying the many small towns across the country that rely on volunteer service to fight fires.

Particularly today, with municipal budgets being continually squeezed to make the most of every dollar, an all-volunteer fire department is a financial necessity to small cities and towns.

It is estimated that as many as 75 percent of the fire-fighters in the United States and Canada are volunteers, also known as "vollies." Volunteer fire fighting in the United States has been around since the country's founding, and the basic idea has changed little over the years: community-minded men and women donate a large chunk of their personal time training together and fighting fires.

The ink on the Declaration of Independence was still wet when city leaders in Philadelphia, New York, and Boston began organizing and operating volunteer fire departments with what was then considered state-of-the-art equipment.

Their modest hand pumpers were a vast improvement over previous methods of colonial fire fighting, which usually meant little more than knocking down adjacent buildings to prevent the spread of fire. The hand pumper and later canvas hoses marked a technological leap in fire fighting for the volunteer.

Shortly before the Civil War, with the large influx of European immigrants, volunteer fire departments began to be divided along ethnic lines. German, Irish, and Italian communities organized their own volunteer fire departments, which became the leading clubs in their neighborhoods. These new volunteers ultimately competed for fire business with the older, established volunteer fire companies. It wasn't uncommon for turf wars to break out between rival volunteer companies, sometimes resembling today's gang wars, except for the sophisticated weaponry.

But weaponry they had. Volunteer firefighters often used fire axes and even water from hoses to battle rival volunteer gangs at the scene of an alarm. These pitched battles became so frequent over the years that officials in large cities grew weary and developed professional departments with budgets for firefighters' salaries. It was an effective strategy, and fire departments became more concerned with fighting flames than rivals.

This trend among large cities could have been the death knell for volunteer departments. Instead, volunteer firefighters responded by becoming more professional in their work; they came to think of their volunteer status as a badge of honor setting them apart from their mercenary professional colleagues.

This book chronicles the progress of the firefighter's equipment, from the glories of the horse-drawn steamer of post–Civil War America to the Super Pumper of the 1960s and today's specialized Haz-mat operations.

Every now and then I use my VCR to watch one of my favorite films, the old sci-fi thriller *Invasion of the Body Snatchers*. It has absolutely nothing to do with fire fighting, but a large part of the movie was filmed in Sierra Madre. In one of its climactic scenes, the air raid horn on top of City Hall blasts away to warn the town's residents of danger. And the memories of my youth come flooding back.

TOP: Horses displayed tremendous agility and speed when pulling a steamer to fire alarms during the pre-motorized era.

BOTTOM: One of the first Maxims ever built was purchased by the Middleboro Fire Department in Massachusetts in 1914. This combination chemical and hose wagon is a Model F.

CHAPTER ONE

1900 — 1920

THERE WAS A CURIOUS PERIOD IN AMERICAN HISTORY, BETWEEN ABOUT 1915 AND 1925, WHEN PEOPLE ON THE STREET IN TOWNS BIG AND SMALL WOULD STOP WHAT THEY WERE DOING, RUSH TO THE CURBSIDE, AND WAVE AFFECTIONATELY AT THE HORSE-DRAWN FIRE ENGINES THUNDERING BY ON THEIR WAY TO AN ALARM.

They knew the era of horse-drawn fire engines was drawing to a close and that they were witnessing the passing of true horsepower. If many of them were sad to think of the horses' imminent retirement, it was nothing compared with how many of the firefighters felt. In the coming years, more than a few of them would quit their prestigious jobs rather than go on without their horses.

Across the nation, the horse had served volunteer and professional fire departments faithfully for more than fifty years. Many firefighters—after overcoming their initial resistance—loved their animals. Teams of two, three, and sometimes four horses could be harnessed in less than three minutes at the onset of an alarm, to come crashing through a fire station's double doors and gallop fiercely to a blaze. Horses seemed to love the thrill of responding to a fire as much as their human counterparts did. Even when teams were retired and sold as surplus to haul milk or ice wagons, the desire to respond to a blaze was still strong. It was not uncommon to have a retired fire horse pulling a delivery wagon show up at an alarm at the same time as a gasoline-powered fire engine—often without its new owner.

But Gottlieb Daimler's invention of the automobile in 1886, along with the development of mass-production techniques by Henry Ford in 1908, made the demise of the horse-drawn fire engine inevitable.

Even though the newfangled machines were noisy, smelly, and at times unreliable, city and county fire officials couldn't ignore the real and significant cost benefits of self-propelled fire apparatus.

During the first two decades of the twentieth century, fire journals kept close tabs of the daily costs of motor-drawn engines for purposes of comparison with horses, and the savings were obvious.

Springfield, Massachusetts, is believed to have been the first city to have a fully motorized fire department, and city officials kept meticulous records. They determined that it cost $1.90 per day to maintain horse-drawn apparatus whereas it cost only 14¢ a day for the self-propelled variety.

Richmond, Virginia, also jumped on the motorized bandwagon in the first decade of the century. It reported that maintaining a gasoline-powered fire engine cost only 13¢ per day, whereas horses costs as much as $2.18 each day.

By 1900, it was evident that the gasoline engine was here to stay. It was only a matter of time before fire departments would become fully motorized. Only love of horses, resistance to change, and the shortsightedness of municipal governments allowed the horse-driven fire engine to remain in use through the 1920s.

For the most part, the fire department brass in hundreds of towns and cities were eager to be rid of the burden of being responsible for the costly maintenance of horses. Professional fire departments, such as New York's, began using horses in the 1860s. Volunteer fire departments were slower to change, but ultimately they, too, began using horses in the 1880s. Dr. Peter Molloy, director of the Hall of Flame Museum in Phoenix, Arizona, explains firefighters' reluctance to switch to horses:

> Volunteers fought horses because no one wanted to take care of them. Horses required a lot of care. And volunteer fire departments were social clubs much like today's Rotary Club. These were middle-class men attempting to raise their image, and mucking

out stalls didn't raise their image. Their reputation was important. But what forced them to use horses was the steamer and heavier equipment.

The steamer, a pump powered by a built-in steam engine, is technically a fire engine because it provides power to send a stream of water into a fire. But very few builders at the time considered using the steamer's engine to propel the apparatus under its own power to an alarm.

San Francisco bears the distinction of introducing the first fire apparatus to move entirely under its own power. It was the fire chief's electric car, purchased in 1901. New York acquired an electric car shortly thereafter.

But the first true gasoline-powered fire engine debuted at the 1898 Paris Salon de l'Automobile. French builder Cambier and Co. developed a two-speed four-cylinder engine that could hit a top speed of 15 kilometers [9.3mi.] per hour. Perhaps the most famous steam-powered engine was purchased in 1894 by the Hartford, Connecticut, fire department from Amoskeag Corporation of the Manchester Locomotive Works in Manchester, New Hampshire.

Probably nothing was more exciting to a young boy than seeing a three-horse team thundering down the street pulling a steam fire engine. This fire unit races through the intersection of 72nd Street and Broadway in New York City around 1910.

THE STEAM ERA

The Silsby Manufacturing Co. brass nameplate on one of its 1879 steam engines. There are only three of these machines left.

As advanced as fire-fighting technology is today, there have been few real improvements in performance over the steam-powered pumpers of the nineteenth century. In terms of water volume and the distance a stream of water can travel, the steamer is very much comparable with today's sophisticated and expensive equipment.

The world's first steam fire engine was built in 1828 by George Braithwaite and John Ericsson, both of London, England. And despite its obvious superiority over manual pumpers, it took three decades before municipalities began to accept fully the steamer into fire-fighting service.

Steam power was the driving force behind the Industrial Revolution, and was the basis of the locomotive, which brought mass transportation to the world. But, manifesting a common resistance to change, civic leaders believed that when it came to fighting fires, nothing could replace the reliability of the brute muscle of men. Besides, the advent of the steam engine threatened to take away vital jobs. Never mind that the steam fire engine could do the job of two dozen men at a fraction of the cost.

Even when Braithwaite and Ericsson's invention proved itself at the infamous Argyll Rooms Opera House fire in London, it still did not change the established philosophy on how to fight a fire. Although considered quaint and archaic today, the steamer of the early nineteenth century was a magnificent innovation, comparable to today's advancements in computer technology. It was exciting, and many people were dazzled by its possibilities, but at the same time it frightened them with its promise of radical change.

Braithwaite and Ericsson's steamer was a 10-horsepower affair with two horizontal cylinders that provided enough pressure to throw 150 gallons [567.8l] of water per minute to a height of 90 feet [27.4m]. It reached working pressure in about twenty minutes and recycled the waste steam from the cylinders through a tube to the feed water tank, raising the water's temperature.

When the Argyll Rooms burst into flames during the harsh winter of 1828–29, manual pumps at the scene froze up. Braithwaite brought his steamer down to the blaze, and it provided a steady stream of water for five hours. Yet firefighters railed against the invention, claiming that it was too powerful for the street's water mains.

The steamer was used again with great success at the Barclay's Brewery blaze. Barclay's management asked Braithwaite to loan them the steamer after the fire. Braithwaite was delighted until he discovered they only wanted the machine to pump beer.

There were some legitimate concerns about the use of the steamer in fighting fires. For one, steam fire engines could pump water at a tremendously fast rate, emptying wells in seconds. Many cities and towns were not prepared for the superior advancement of the steam engine until they constructed cisterns under streets. Another problem was that steam engines were extremely heavy and could not be moved quickly. The heft of a steam engine was particularly apparent when firefighters attempted to navigate muddy streets only to become hopelessly bogged down.

Braithwaite was devastated by the shortsightedness of town officials over the use of his invention. But by the 1850s—as the invention was being perfected—enthusiasm for the contraption began to pick up steam.

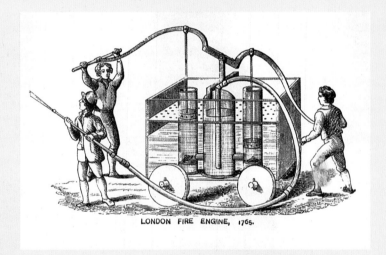

LONDON FIRE ENGINE, 1765.

Steam fire engines were complicated mechanisms. According to Hans Halberstadt, author of *The American Fire Engine*, a working steamer had to be kept warm. Most engines were equipped with quick water disconnects to keep the boiler water hot. Placed on a grate at the base of the engine was kindling soaked in kerosene and several pieces of coal. When the alarm sounded, the kindling was ignited and the water lines disconnected. This took only a few seconds, and was easily done while the horses were being hitched.

The water level—observed through a sight glass—had to be maintained, with all vents and petcocks for the steam part of the pump open while the metal of the boiler was warmed up. The firefighter had to monitor the water pressure gauge until it achieved a working pressure of about 55 pounds per square inch. The valve was then opened to allow steam into the pump. Water would then vent from the drains. When the water stopped, the valves and petcocks were closed, and the pump began to build up pressure. All

of this occurred while firefighters were racing to the scene. By the time they arrived at the blaze, the boiler fire was roaring, and the pump was ready to put water to fire. Firefighters had to consult a checklist of up to forty items to maintain a successful pumper.

The first big break for steamers came on January 1, 1853, at a Cincinnati, Ohio, competition between a hand-pumping crew from the Union Fire Company and a steam-powered pumper. Union Fire volunteers managed to get water on the blaze first, and achieved a height of 200 feet [60.96m], but they were exhausted within a half hour. The steam pumper, however, produced a 225-foot [68.6m] stream, and, needless to say, did not get tired.

By the outbreak of the American Civil War, the steam fire engine was beginning to earn respect. Several steam fire engine manufacturers began popping up. Seneca Falls, New York, became "The Fire Engine Capital of the World," with a number of makers opening there, thanks largely to the State Barge Canal that ran through the city. The first

OPPOSITE TOP: A crude hand-pumped London fire engine in 1765 required two men to operate the pump and a third to direct the hose. The pump provided about as much pressure as a garden hose, and proved impractical for large-scale fire fighting.
OPPOSITE BOTTOM: This early version of a steam fire engine was designed in 1840 by John Ericsson of London. The engine proved to be a huge success. Earlier steam engines by Ericsson and his partner, George Braithwaite, were met with derision by the fire-fighting community because they were perceived as taking away jobs.
LEFT: A 1910 Ahrens-Continental steam engine delivered to the Memphis Fire Department.

manufacturer in Seneca Falls was Pain & Caldwell, which set up shop in 1839. They were followed by the Silsby Manufacturing Company in 1861, which would survive to become a leader in the industry, thanks to its popular rotary engine. Silsby engines were also a big hit in Philadelphia, which replaced its whole fleet of steamers with forty-one Silsbys between 1886 and 1897. Also settling in Seneca Falls were Rumsey & Company in 1864; Gleason & Bailey in 1884; and the American Fire Engine Company in 1891. Rumsey became well known for its oddly shaped "piano-style" Badger engine, which was used in the Chicago fire of 1871.

The Button Fire Engine Company began building its steam engines in 1862, and sold its first one to the city of Battle Creek, Michigan. Over a period of thirty years, despite producing a total of only about one hundred steamers, Button came to be highly respected in the industry.

In England, James C. Merryweather developed his steamer, the single-cylinder Deluge, which developed 30 horsepower with a bore and stroke of 9 by 15 inches [22.9cm by 38.1cm].

The Deluge was entered in the steam engine trials at the Great Exhibition of 1862 in London's Hyde Park, where it won first in its class. A steamer manufactured by Shand Mason took the small-engine class honors. The Deluge was initially sold to a private fire brigade, then sold to the city of Lyons, France, in 1870.

Merryweather followed with a bigger and more powerful machine, the Torrent, and then the Sutherland in 1863. The Sutherland, equipped with twin steam cylinders and capable of sending a jet of water 170 feet [51.8m], captured top honors at the 1863 Crystal Palace competition in England.

Steam fire engines continued to be manufactured at least until 1916. By 1930, nearly all horse-drawn steamers had been retired, and by 1940 most of the motorized steam apparatus had also left active service, though a small number were kept on as steam generators, used for heating fire stations or thawing out frozen hydrants at the scene of an alarm. During World War II, because the steam fire engines were made with a large amount of brass, many of them were collected and destroyed in scrap drives.

RIGHT: Already an antique in 1935, when this picture was taken, a Merryweather steamer gets a thorough polishing from firemen in Brighton, England, in preparation for a Jubilee Day procession.
OPPOSITE: A common sight in middle America was men and boys running pell-mell after a horse-drawn steam fire engine as it went clanging through the streets belching smoke.

Considered the largest steam engine of its day, the apparatus jetted a stream of water nearly 350 feet [106.7m] and could reach a then-astounding speed of 31 mph [49.6kph].

It was during this time, approaching the turn of the century, that James Compton Merryweather, of Greenwich, England, was seriously considering the benefits of steam-powered pumps and propulsion. Merryweather had already developed the steam-powered Greenwich Gem when, in 1899, he produced the Merryweather steamer, which moved under its own power at a whopping 20 mph [32kph].

Three years later, Merryweather developed his legendary Fire King self-propelled steamer. The Fire King was produced between 1902 and 1918 and featured six basic models ranging from a low-priced 300-gallon [1,135.5l] version to the deluxe 1000-gallon [3,785l] model. These versions could be ordered with coke or oil-fired boilers. Fire Kings were exported around the world and offered options such as iron-spoked wheels.

In 1904, the Paris fire department puchased a steamer similar to the Fire King, built by the French firm Weyher et Richemonde. This model included a 30-horsepower compound steam engine that had a pumping capacity of 575 gallons [12,176.4l] per minute (gpm). Its top speed was 15 mph [24kph].

That same year, Merryweather constructed the first gasoline-powered fire engine that would see regular service. The fire engine came equipped with a 30-horsepower engine that was used both for propulsion and to power the 250-gpm [1946.3l] pump. It also carried 180 feet [54.9m] of hose and a 60-gallon [227.1l] chemical tank.

Gottlieb Daimler's company in Germany was responsible for building a series of electric-powered chassis for fire fighting. The electric motors were built into the front wheels. Other German builders of electric fire engines were Flader, which used equipment manufactured by Namag, and Protos, which used the Siemens-Schubert electrical propulsion system.

By 1901, a number of gasoline-powered vehicles hit European roads. The Adler, for example, was equipped with seating for four firefighters, a small pump and hose reel, short scaling ladders, and fire hooks. Other manufacturers that followed Adler were Opel, Bussing, Hansa-Lloyd, Durkopp, Stoewer, and Magirus.

In Europe, massive urban development created very narrow streets and tall buildings, and the difficulty of navigating these cities made the search for technical advancements in fire engines urgent. For this reason, new fire-fighting technology was rapidly adopted by European fire departments. In the United States, on the other hand, most departments didn't feel an urgent need to develop self-propelled fire engines quickly, although the threat of fire to structures was four times greater in the United States than in Europe. As a consequence, American fire departments as a rule kept their horse-drawn apparatus longer than their European counterparts did.

Nonetheless, the momentum for change was building, and by the turn of the century, several commercial truck and fire engine manufacturers emerged to reshape the way fires were fought.

FORD

Perhaps the most reliable and inexpensive fire engine on the road during the first two decades of the century were the Ford Model T and its 1-ton [0.9t] truck version, the Model TT.

With its debut in 1908, the Ford Model T enjoyed a successful nineteen-year lifespan unparalleled by any other vehicle. Independent manufacturers sold kits for converting early Model T cars into trucks. These kits converted the rear wheels into sprockets and linked them by chains to a pair of new rear wheels (with solid rubber tires) on an extended frame.

During this period, Fords were ubiquitous. Ford dealers dotted communities from one end of the country to the other. Ford cars and replacement parts were cheap and plentiful. The high ground clearance of these vehicles made them

**OPPOSITE: An example of the hybrid fire engine: a Christie tractor attached to a steam fire engine. This one is Engine 258 of the New York City Fire Department working on an oil company blaze in Brooklyn on September 13, 1919.
BELOW: This fire engine is typical of the many appliances built on Ford Model T chassis during the early part of the century.**

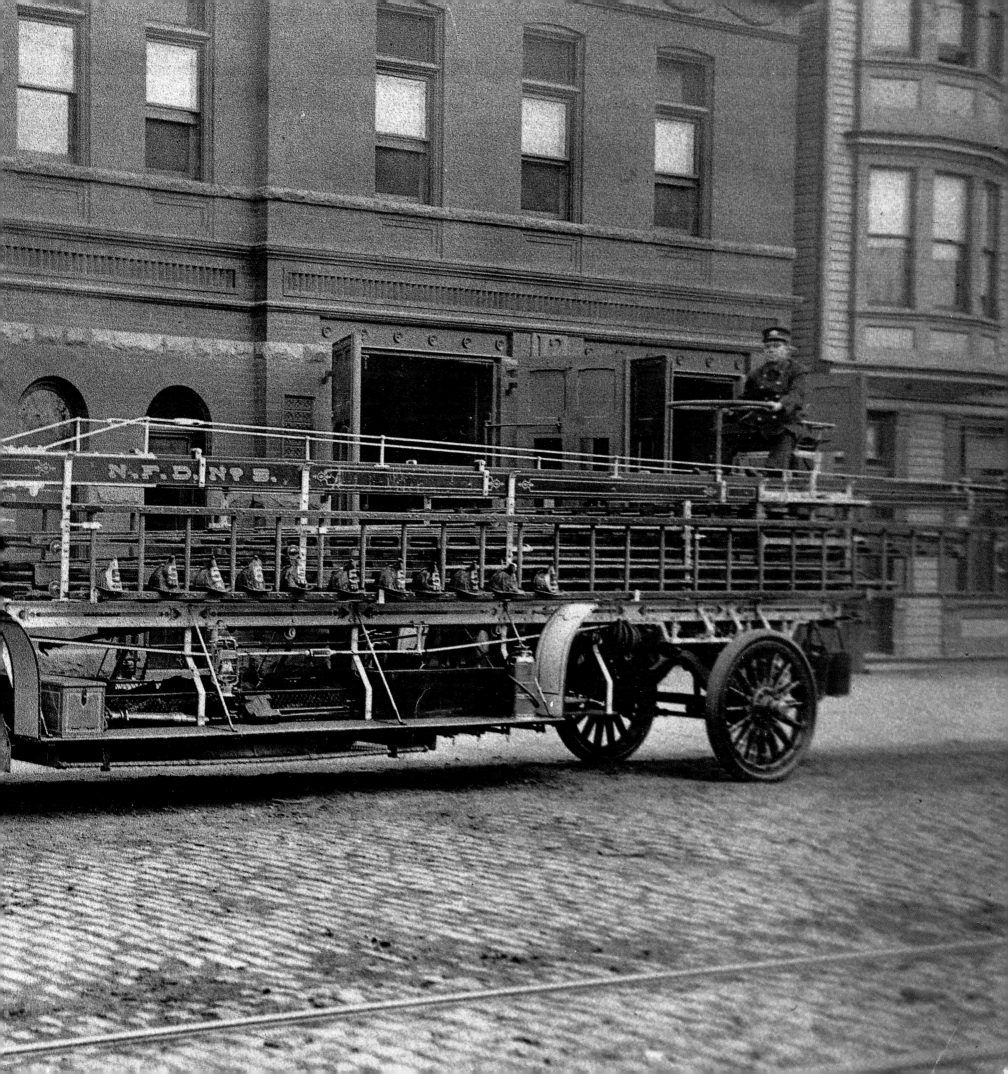

ideal at a time when the country's road system was relatively primitive. Many fire departments in rural areas would purchase a Model T at a very low cost and then buy a third-party kit to convert it to a fire engine, usually with a twin-tank chemical unit.

The Ford Motor Co. recognized the popularity of these hybrids—not to mention the fact they were not making any money on the kits—and introduced its 1-ton [0.9t] Model TT in 1917. The truck sold for about $600 and instantly became a popular fire-fighting machine.

But for all its innovations, the Ford Motor Co. was a relative latecomer to the fire-fighting scene. A converted Model T could perform quite well in a community of a few hundred or even a few thousand. But with urbanization and the subsequent demand for state-of-the-art equipment came the requirement that fire-fighting apparatus be manufactured and sold on a larger scale.

Even before motorized fire engines came onto the scene, there was a need for smaller manufacturers to band together to meet the demands of new technology in fire fighting.

Many manufacturers also wanted to protect themselves from unfair competition.

AMERICAN LAFRANCE

The leading builder of steam fire engines in the late nineteenth century was the Amoskeag Company of New York. Amoskeag began building steam fire engines in 1859 and established the standard in steamers between 1872 and 1908. Amoskeag built more than one thousand machines, which came in various sizes and types depending on the client's requirements.

Other smaller concerns struggled to keep up with Amoskeag. The Silsby Company of Seneca Falls, New York; Clapp & Jones of Hudson, New York; the Button Fire Engine Works; and Chris Ahrens, later of Ahrens-Fox, made up the rest of the competition. All of these companies pioneered significant advancements in fire-fighting techniques.

Silsby, which began making steam engines in 1856, developed the rotary pump, which was said to produce less

PREVIOUS PAGE:
With motorized apparatus becoming more common every day, the Newark, New Jersey, fire department still continued to use horses to pull some equipment. Truck Company No. 5 consisted of a three-horse team pulling a 75-foot [22.5m] American LaFrance aerial hook and ladder. It was put into service on January 11, 1909. This photograph was taken circa 1912.
RIGHT: This is a more elaborate Christie creation, a tractor designed to blend in with a steam engine. Constructed in 1911, it is one of the more beautiful examples of fire-engine workmanship. It was sold to the Plainview, New Jersey, fire department.

friction loss in the hose than the standard piston pump. Clapp & Jones produced about 600 steam engines between 1862 and 1891 and specialized in vertical boilers.

In 1891, Silsby, Clapp & Jones, Button, and Ahrens joined under a single umbrella to form the American Fire Engine Company, partially in an attempt to compete against the likes of the fire-fighting equipment giant Amoskeag, which had merged in 1872 with another big name of the era, Manchester Locomotive Works.

Ten years later, fire equipment manufacturer LaFrance joined American to become the International Fire Engine Company. Also included in the new merger were smaller makers: Thos. Manning Jr. & Company, Rumsey, Gleason & Bailey, and Chas. T. Holloway; and fire extinguisher manufacturers Chicago Fire Extinguisher Company, F. E. Babcock Company, and the Macomber Chemical Fire Extinguisher Company.

The company, under the International moniker, attempted in 1903 to establish a factory in Chicago Heights, Illinois, only to collapse in a financial morass. It reemerged under a reorganization plan as the American LaFrance Fire Engine Company, soon to become known as a major player in the burgeoning fire-fighting equipment industry.

But American LaFrance's first attempt to build a gasoline-powered truck rig failed. It was introduced in 1907 as a 30-horsepower chemical wagon, ordered by the Boston Fire Department. Unfortunately, it was rejected and returned unused. Three years later, American LaFrance successfully sold the Boston department a combination chemical and hose wagon.

The company continued manufacturing hand pumpers until 1910 before turning to a rotary-gear system a year later. The Type 10 and Type 12 models offered pumping speeds of 500 gpm [1,892.5l] and 750 gpm [2,838.8l], respectively.

Among other American LaFrance fire engines were the 75-horsepower Type 31 tractor and the smaller Type 40 model that was offered with pumping speeds of either 250 or 350 gallons [946.2l or 1,324.8l] per minute. In 1916, the company sent a Type 40 junior pumper, with a 350 gpm [1,324.8l] rotary pump (nearly identical to the 1878 Silsby steam pumper) and a large hose bed, to the farm town of Paxton, Illinois. During World War I, another pumper built by American LaFrance was sent to Mamaroneck, New York. The department there used the 600-gpm [2,271l] pumper with 40-gallon [151.4l] chemical tank until about 1950, a testament to its exceptional durability.

AHRENS-FOX

In 1891, Ahrens, Button, Clapp & Jones, and Silsby were consolidated to form the American Fire Engine Company. In 1904 there was another merger, joining the American Fire Engine Company and the International Fire Engine Company to create the American-LaFrance Fire Engine Company.

Dissatisfied with the new management, Chris Ahrens, with his sons and sons-in-law, resigned that same year to form a new company. He called it the Cincinnati Engine & Pump Works, but filed suit to regain the right to use the Ahrens name. One of Ahrens' sons-in-law was Charles Fox, who was already the premier designer of boilers for steam

ABOVE: The glittering beauty of this 1879 steam engine belongs to an era long past.
BELOW: A 65-foot American-LaFrance Type 31 ladder and hose truck serving the town of Parkersburg, West Virginia.

pumpers. At the turn of the century, the boiler on virtually every steamer in the United States was built under one or more of Fox's patents.

In 1905, one week after winning the suit to use the Ahrens name, the company delivered its first steamer, the Continental. In 1910, the company was renamed Ahrens-Fox, and Charles Fox was elected president. He continued to refine his designs, culminating in 1919 with the introduction of the Model J, the first modern triple combination pumper. It was a masterpiece of technical achievement and artistry, sporting a massive solid bronze piston pump and bright nickel-plated air dome mounted directly in front of the radiator.

Considered the Cadillac of fire engines up until the company's demise in 1957, the Ahrens-Fox was not a vehicle for a city with a tight pocketbook. These machines were very expensive. As a result, only about 1,500 were manufactured between 1911 and 1957, a mere handful compared to production totals for Mack and American LaFrance.

CHRISTIE

J. Walter Christie specialized in front-wheel drive tractors, but he played a vital part in the transition from horse-drawn fire apparatus to gasoline-powered engines. Much of his work between about 1897 and 1915 focused on fitting horse-drawn appliances to gasoline engines.

Although very crude, these machines were quite effective, and Christie attempted to incorporate many of the features offered by American LaFrance. They were solid and bulky, usually with a ninety-horsepower engine mounted in the front of the front-wheel drives. A typical Christie could pull up to 18 tons [16.3t].

One model, on display at the Hall of Flame Museum, is an 1899 LaFrance steam fire engine equipped with a Christie engine. Between 1910 and 1925, Christie equipped more than a thousand horse-drawn steamers with such tractors. Also on display at the Hall of Flame is a Champion water tower, designed to pump between 1,000 and 3,000 gpm [3,785l and

RIGHT: A typical view of a nineteenth-century fire station.
BELOW: A crude but effective hand-pumper, still in service with a New England volunteer fire department as late as 1910.

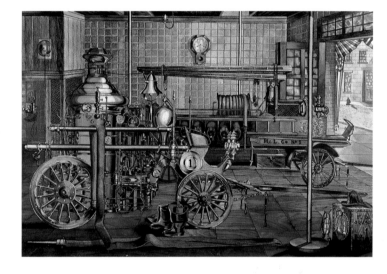

11,355l], that was originally horse-drawn. In 1915, the Toledo, Ohio, fire department motorized it with a Christie.

MACK

The Mack brothers began their career in transportation when Augustus Mack became a clerk for the Christian Fellesen Wagon Factory. One year later he was joined by his brother Jack. When Fellesen retired in 1893, the brothers assumed control of the company and renamed it Mack. In 1894, they were joined by their eldest brother, William.

In 1901, Jack took his first ride in an automobile, and he saw the future of transportation. The brothers focused their energies on truck and bus manufacturing, building their first bus in the winter of 1902. Their second bus was manufactured in 1904. One year later Mack introduced larger heavy-duty trucks, identified as the Senior line, and smaller versions called the Junior line. In 1911, Mack pro-

duced its first pumper, a Senior line chassis equipped with a Gould's pump. Mack's first ladder truck was sold in 1912 to the Resolute Hook & Ladder Co., No. 1, of Morristown, New Jersey. By this time the company had outgrown its Brooklyn factory and moved to Allentown, Pennsylvania.

Mack initially farmed out its body-building work to independent contractors, but in 1914, it began to construct its own. That same year Mack introduced the small AB model chassis, and then the Model AC Bulldog, with a body style heavily influenced by French truck designs of the day.

The AB was the company's first standardized high-volume vehicle. It was used primarily for light and medium fire duty as either a pumper, a chemical wagon, or a hose wagon. It came equipped with either worm or exposed chain drive, wood spoke wheels, and solid rubber tires. More than 50,000 of these machines came out of Mack factories between 1914 and 1937.

The Rutherford, New Jersey, fire department took delivery of this Mack Model AB in 1920 as a city service ladder truck. The AB, heavily influenced by French truck designs, was Mack's first standardized high-volume vehicle, and it was an incredibly popular postwar truck for many municipalities.

K-2398

The Model AC was affectionately dubbed the Bulldog by World War I doughboys for the pugnacious appearance of its sloping nose. Hundreds of Bulldogs were pressed into war service. Their 40-horsepower engines with a 5-by-6 bore and stroke proved extremely reliable under even the most arduous circumstances. At the close of the war, cities scrambled to purchase the war surplus trucks at bargain prices. The city of Chicago bought five AC Bulldogs and immediately converted them to pumpers and hose and chemical wagons. The city of Baltimore purchased nearly two dozen Bulldogs to complement its motorized fleet.

More than 40,000 AC Bulldogs were manufactured through 1938. In 1919, Mack began fitting the AC chassis with a Northern fire pump with speeds of 500 and 600 gpm [1.892.5l and 2.271l].

MAXIM

The Maxim Motor Company was a small operation founded on the belief that by making only slight modifications in fire-fighting apparatus, it would be possible to greatly improve its effectiveness.

Founded by Carlton Maxim in 1888 in Middleboro, Massachusetts, the company produced its first fire engine in 1914 on a Thomas Flier chassis. In 1916, Maxim began to build pumpers on its own chassis.

The company prospered during the war years, and by 1918 it was offering a complete line of fire engines.

Maxim's success was largely based on its development of the Magirus, a compact aerial ladder that proved extremely useful in the small, confining streets of European cities. Maxim produced a line of sturdy ladders that were so durable that Mack—the epitome of ruggedness—equipped its own rigs with them.

SEAGRAVE

Alone among manufacturers of fire-fighting equipment, the Seagrave Company managed to bring a sense of elegance and style to the design of its wagons, while also introducing numerous technical innovations that quickly set new standards for the industry.

In 1912, Seagrave developed the centrifugal pump and the pressure regulator, and in 1915, its unique self-contained auxiliary cooling system was introduced. These inventions marked the beginning of a series of engineering firsts unmatched by any other maker.

Frederic S. Seagrave founded his company during the post–Civil War industrial revolution in Detroit, and by 1881, he had secured his first patent, for a trussed ladder. Over the next twenty years, he was granted another five patents associated with his innovative ladder.

By 1891, Seagrave was having difficulty attracting investors in Detroit, where iron products for railcars and steam engines attracted the big money. He found that Columbus, Ohio, offered a better climate for investors who were eager to put their money into the wagon business. With its shorter winters, Columbus also offered a better climate for drying the paint on Seagrave's wagons, which sometimes took months.

At the turn of the century, Seagrave began to set his sights on motorized apparatus. Automobiles were beginning to dot the roadway, but Seagrave recognized that a stronger chassis than that found on horseless carriages was needed for useful motorized fire-fighting equipment.

Between 1905 and 1909, Seagrave purchased air-cooled 36-horsepower engines from automaker Frayer-Miller and placed them on a chassis that was reinforced to handle the weight of fire apparatus. In 1908, he introduced the country's first tractor-trailer aerial ladder rig. A special tractor powered by a 90-horsepower air-cooled four-cylinder engine hauled a trailer carrying the ladders and hoses. It had a 130-inch [330.2cm] wheelbase with an overall length of 53 feet [16.2m] on top of 40-inch [101.6cm] tires. To stop this massive vehicle, the driver had to press the foot brake to apply the external brake pads while using a hand lever for the internal brake shoes. Seagrave also produced water-cooled units, designated WC models. A massive 75-foot [22.9m] air-cooled version was shipped to Vancouver, British Columbia.

When the Riverside, California, fire department abandoned its horse-drawn fleet in favor of motorized appliances, it turned to Seagrave. On September 15, 1909, the city purchased a Seagrave self-propelled combination hose wagon and chemical engine for $4,750. It was white with gold trim, and it was used to pull the department's steamer, which had previously been pulled by Chub, Spike, Nig, and a handful of their equine friends. These dedicated firefighters were retired (losing one's job because of automation in the workplace is nothing new). In 1912, the department purchased two more Seagraves, and in the 1920s it added American LaFrance fire engines to its inventory.

In 1911, Seagrave introduced three important innovations: an aerial ladder truck with a straight frame, the Model AC-80 straight hose wagon, and a new truck with an auto-

motive-style hood. That same year, Howard B. Spain and Julius F. Stone, who was the chairman of the Board of Trustees for Ohio State University and director of the Ohio National Bank, purchased the Seagrave Company. Spain later became president of the company.

In 1913, Seagrave made waves with the introduction of its stylish gable-type hood, which ran through 1926. Seagrave's fire engines now had a level of panache that could not be matched by its more spartan and utilitarian competition.

During this period, Seagrave developed a new centrifugal pump—the Manistee B—that would serve Seagrave engines for the next five decades. These pumps were heavier and more expensive than previous versions, but they could generate pumping speeds of 750 and 1,000 gpm [2,838.8l and 3,785l].

Along with the new pump came styling changes. The pump control panel and gauges were placed just below the driver's seat, establishing a trend that still persists among nearly all fire engine manufacturers.

In 1917, Seagrave delivered its first motorized water tower, a 65-foot [19.8m] model. It went to Saint Paul on a straight-frame chassis with a rear-mounted mast.

PETER PIRSCH & SONS

In 1892, the Simmons Bed & Mattress Company in Kenosha, Wisconsin, was consumed by fire while the city's firefighters struggled futilely to free their equipment from the thick mud in which it had become stuck. Fire Chief James S. Barr was desperate for a way to avoid a repetition of the disaster.

Barr recognized that what he needed was effective and powerful transportation to haul heavy fire-fighting equipment. He found his answer in Nicholas Pirsch. A native of Bavaria, Pirsch had been building wagons since the early 1850s, and in 1857, he founded the Nicholas Pirsch Wagon and Carriage Plant.

Pirsch's son, Peter, grew up with a passion for fire fighting, and he became a member of the James S. Barr Hook & Ladder Company of the Kenosha Volunteer Fire Department. His ambitions went beyond merely continuing the success and traditions of his father's fire equipment company. He wanted to be the man to bring fire-fighting technology into the twentieth century with an entirely new and modern line of state-of-the-art equipment. In 1898, he deliv-

It wasn't uncommon during the early years of motorized fire engines for builders to use chassis from other manufacturers for their own fire engines. One such builder was Peter Pirsch of Kenosha, Wisconsin. This 1907 Pirsch combination was placed on a Rambler chassis.

ered on his first promise to the Kenosha Fire Department, with a horse-drawn hook and ladder truck that featured multiple ladders and a compartment for hoses.

Kenosha purchased its first fire engine from Pirsch in 1907, becoming only the fourth city in the country—after Springfield, Massachusetts; Joplin, Missouri; and Detroit—to own a gasoline-powered self-propelled fire engine.

One year later, Peter Pirsch introduced the Pirsch Patent Hose Shutoff and Door Opener. But his emphasis continued to be the development of fire engines with up-to-date technology. He still produced horse-drawn equipment such as the two-horse combination Hose and Chemical Wagon produced in 1909, but his hook and ladder combinations were considered truly awesome. His company manufactured a thirty-meter straight-frame aerial ladder that gained considerable popularity during the 1920s.

Although credited with numerous fire-fighting innovations, Pirsch was relatively late in emerging with its first pumper. In 1916 it produced a triple combination pumper that was built on a White Motor Company truck chassis, which was delivered to Creston, Iowa.

NOTT

The W. S. Nott Company of Minneapolis produced a line of reliable pumpers that gained favorable reviews from the New York City Fire Department in the years leading up to World War I.

A maker of steam apparatus since 1879, Nott was a steady contributor in motorized equipment by 1912. Nott produced Universal fire engines that were larger and more streamlined compared with competitors of the day. In 1915, New York City operated two 500-gpm [1,892.5l] Nott triple combination pumpers and a combination pumper and hose wagon.

SMALLER MAKERS

During the early part of the century, there were several other companies that contributed greatly to the development of fire-fighting equipment.

The Boyer Fire Apparatus Company built a series of chemical carts that were treasured by small towns and large industrial plants. A typical Boyer chemical cart constructed before World War I consisted of a 40-gallon [151.4l] tank that was easy to operate and refuel.

Waterous Engine Works was equally popular for its chemical carts, but it also offered a hand- or horse-drawn pumper that was quite popular.

Founded in Saint Paul, it began manufacturing horse-drawn gasoline-powered pumpers in 1898. In 1906 it developed a 350-gpm [1,324.8l] pumper that was easier to operate and maintain than a steam pumper. It could be drawn either by horses or by hand. It typified the many unusual hybrids that came on the market during this early era as part of the transition from horse-drawn to motorized appliances.

Waterous also provided two-tank chemical carts that had the fire-fighting capacity of about twenty-five handheld fire extinguishers.

The first two decades of the twentieth century were in many ways a period of trial and error, as engineers and designers searched for the best methods to incorporate automotive technology into fire-fighting apparatus. As a result, there was a wild diversity of models and designs, with many peculiar hybrids appearing briefly on the scene. During the next two decades, with the technology becoming more standardized, the emphasis turned to building bigger and more powerful machines and to introducing innovative and attention-getting styling.

TOP: The Mount Vernon, Washington, fire department displays a 1920 American LaFrance 750-gpm [2,838.8l] Type 12 pumper.

BOTTOM: A Howe-Lambert piston pump is mounted on this Ford Model T. The Howe Fire Apparatus Co. of Anderson, Indiana, assembled the equipment. The Lambert three-piston, or triplex, pump had, with some modifications, a capacity of about 300 gpm [1,135.5l] at 120 pounds [54.4kg] of pump pressure. Howe produced these pumps well into the 1950s. This photograph is circa 1917.

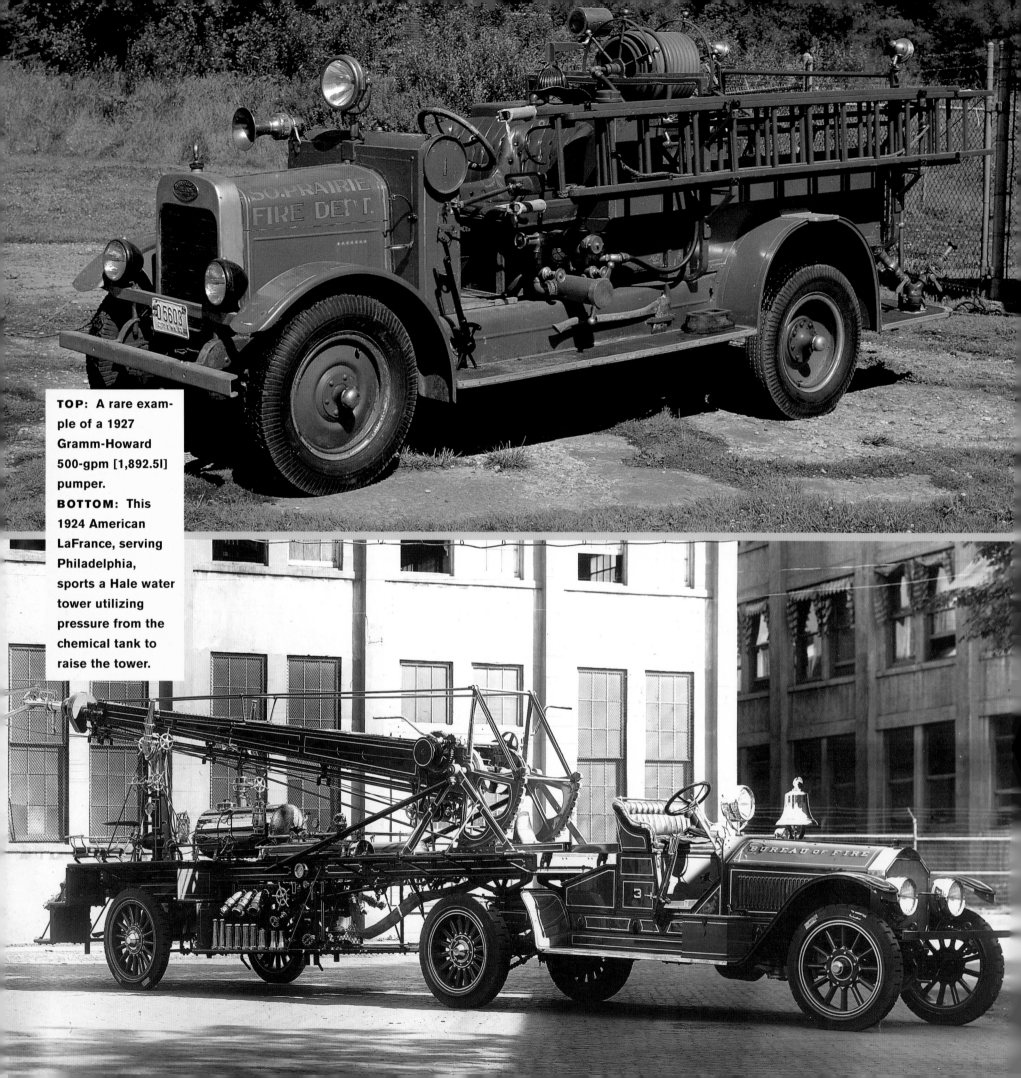

TOP: A rare example of a 1927 Gramm-Howard 500-gpm [1,892.5l] pumper.

BOTTOM: This 1924 American LaFrance, serving Philadelphia, sports a Hale water tower utilizing pressure from the chemical tank to raise the tower.

CHAPTER TWO

1921
1940

AFTER 1920, MANUFAC-
TURERS OF FIRE-FIGHTING
EQUIPMENT BEGAN SUB-
SCRIBING TO THE THEORY
THAT BIGGER IS BETTER
AND PRODUCED BEHE-
MOTHS THAT ROARED
DOWN THE ROADWAY WITH
AN AUTHORITY NO OTHER
VEHICLE COULD MATCH.

The Roaring Twenties witnessed Duesenberg, Lincoln, and Cadillac making tremendous strides in automobile technology. Duesenberg, in particular, pioneered the heavy use of aluminum, introducing aluminum firewalls to replace wooden ones, and aluminum engine parts to reduce weight. Pneumatic tires replaced solid ones, and shaft drives slowly replaced the archaic chain drive.

New fire engines also included all-wheel brakes, electric lights, air cleaners, turn indicators, shock absorbers, pressurized lubrication, and enclosed gears.

Local fire departments, however, were just as resistant to change as ever. In part, this stemmed from the fact that firefighters were a clannish, traditional lot, but it must also be remembered that they regularly put their lives in danger and needed to be able to depend on their equipment. Unsurprisingly, they tended to feel safer using equipment with which they were familiar, rather than entrusting their lives to new and unproven devices. However, several factors conspired to change this institutional resistance to new automotive technology.

When the United States entered World War I in 1917, many firefighters put down their hoses and axes and picked up rifles. The military was training hundreds of men to drive trucks for the European campaign. For the first time, servicemen could obtain the grade of chauffeur and become expert drivers. By the end of the war, there was a large corps of men who felt comfortable driving a massive rig.

Firefighters also witnessed a slow move by manufacturers to make their rigs into things of beauty rather than functional yet unattractive machines. Driving one of these new sensual big red machines down the street attracted a lot of attention. Firefighters navigating horse-drawn steam engines had always stopped folks dead in their tracks, but a gleaming Ahrens-Fox fire engine—equipped with huge front-mounted piston pumper, water tank, hoses and ladders, powered by a 1,160-cubic-inch [7,080cc] engine—was a real showstopper.

Truck sales began to take off. By 1920, there were 321,789 trucks sold in the country, pushing total truck registrations over the 1 million mark. By 1929, 3.3 million trucks were registered. Chevrolet sold 160,959 trucks that year, and Ford sold a whopping 223,425.

SEAGRAVE

As the new decade began, Seagrave started to broaden its range of equipment. It expanded and improved its line of ladder trucks, and began offering the tractor-drawn rigs in lengths of 65, 75, and 85 feet [19.8, 22.9, and 25.9m].

PREVIOUS PAGE:
New York City firefighters battle a second-floor blaze in a loft building that housed the Grossman & Oser Mattress Co. The building at 622 Water Street was a total loss, but no employees were killed or injured.
RIGHT: A 1925 750-gpm [2,838.8l] Seagrave pumper serving the Anaheim, California, fire department.

Seagrave also recognized that people were becoming more demanding when it came to vehicle design. By 1921, Seagrave introduced its cast aluminum firewall and rounded hood and radiator grille, becoming the first fire engine manufacturer to emphasize design. From the cowl forward, the new machines had a distinct streamlined look, with free-flowing lines and fewer angles. Smooth gull-wing fenders replaced the square, iron-reinforced prewar fenders. The boxy look was disappearing.

Other fire engine manufacturers did not exactly rush to follow the streamlining trend. Many fire departments were afraid that introducing radical new designs like Seagrave's would make their existing fleets seem dated. Seagrave managers, meanwhile, found that by continuing to offer their older models they could keep their more conservative customers while enhancing their reputation for innovative, up-to-the-minute designs.

Seagrave prospered during the economic boom of the twenties. As an exclusive fire engine maker, it rose to be perhaps the most stable company in the industry, with three hundred employees in 1925, churning out up to 200 vehicles a year. In 1929, before the stock market crash, Seagrave expanded its Columbus plant and went international by opening its own Canadian factory.

In 1923, Seagrave introduced its first true full line of fire engines. Responding to demands by small fire departments for a smaller, less expensive unit, the company produced the Suburbanite pumper, powered by a six-cylinder Continental engine and delivering 350 gpm [1,324.8l] . Many Suburbanites were placed on Ford Model A commercial chassis. The 70-horsepower six-cylinder Continental was offered until 1931, when it was replaced by the 90-horsepower Hercules XYC engine. It stood less than 6 feet [1.8m] tall and weighed a mere 6,700 pounds [3,041.8kg]. The average price tag for these little runabouts was about $6,600. In elaborate advertisements, Seagrave boasted of the Suburbanite that "the centrifugal pump is guaranteed to deliver rated capacity, barring abuse, for 10 years."

Seagrave was surprised to find that the Suburbanite was popular with larger departments as well as small ones. The new pumper was the perfect machine for handling smaller emergencies.

In 1925, the Detroit Fire Department took delivery of two Suburbanite pumpers and two service ladder trucks; the following year it purchased two additional ladder trucks.

The Colton, California, fire department still has possession of a 1926 Seagrave triple combination Suburbanite pumper equipped with the standard 350-gpm [1,324.8l]

ABOVE: A view of the cockpit of a classic fire engine owned by the Croton Point, New York, fire department. LEFT: A combination chemical and hose fire engine from Maxim on a Thomas Flier chassis. This was delivered to the Ansonia, Connecticut, fire department.

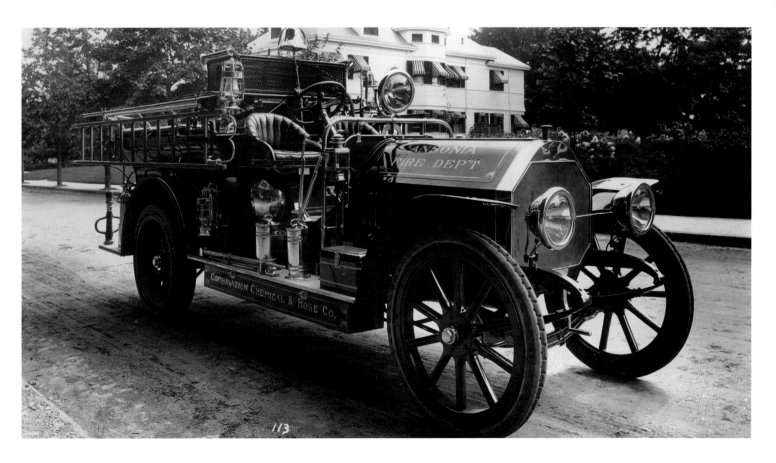

THE STREAMLINE ERA

Traditionalists who believed in fighting fires with good old-fashioned muscle, American firefighters were always slow to respond to changing times, especially if changes threatened to make their job easier or safer. They liked the idea of really working for a living, so it isn't really surprising that firefighters balked at the idea of riding in the safety of an enclosed cab.

Fire equipment manufacturers, however, were eager to follow the rest of the automotive industry by producing new lines of sleekly streamlined fire engines to carry crews to alarms in the latest style.

Despite the Depression, automakers were busy creating stylish streamlined cars. Errett Lobban Cord was perhaps the leader in this trend, producing the Duesenberg, Cord, and Auburn. Chrysler had the streamlined AirFlow,

and Pierce-Arrow offered its Silver Arrow. These two innovative cars set the standard for what cars would look like over the next two decades.

It stands to reason that truck makers would follow automobile styling trends. By the mid-1930s, trucks—and fire engines, of course—sported chrome grilles, two-piece V-shaped windshields, closed cabs, separate parking lights on top of fenders, and more gauges on the instrument panel. Later, these trucks would integrate headlights into fenders and offer cab-over-engine models.

Truck and fire engine enthusiasts were quick to praise American truck makers for their quick adaptation streamlined styling. Unfortunately for the fan of American know-how and innovation, however, it turns out that European fire engine makers were first on the block with streamlined design.

The new trend of designing fire engines in a sleek streamlined style was as much a response to safety concerns as to aesthetics. Like their horse-drawn predecessors, fire trucks were initially quite high, with narrow wheels. Slippery roads proved dangerous and often these rigs, laden with heavy equipment, would overturn. This was especially true in Europe, where the older cities have narrower, steeper streets than in the United States. A slippery

Elegance has always been the hallmark of American LaFrance fire engines, and this 400 Series coupe is no exception. Reflecting the design trends of the streamline era, this 1938 750-gpm [2,838.8l] pumper sports a brightly polished radiator and an enclosed cab. It belonged to the Brigham City, Utah, fire department.

road could easily sway equipment and crew members about until somebody was pitched over the side. Despite firefighters' indifference to danger, European designers began to make modest alterations to improve safety, such as adding windshields and doors.

In 1932, Leyland, the British manufacturer, delivered its Cub KSX to the Borough of Abingood. It allowed crew members to sit inside the body and had a twin axle rear that came equipped with removable tracks over the rear wheels for negotiating soft or muddy roadways. In Germany, where manufacturers had long been concerned about crew protection, several fire rigs with doors to protect firefighters were on the road in the early 1930s. Virtually no rigs in the United States displayed these safety concerns at that time.

German manufacturers produced the enclosed rig as early as 1910. One maker designed a large van that wasn't equipped with a windshield and carried only three crew members. The pump was placed under the floor, and there were large lockers to store equipment. Although Germany led the industry in safety, England and France were far ahead of their neighbor in styling.

Another maker, Magirus, designed a 3,000-pound [1,362kg] enclosed-cab truck in 1921 that featured pneumatic tires and used a canvas sheet to cover its equipment on a half-body.

One of the first successful examples of a fully enclosed rig was a 1929 effort by British firefighters. A driver with the Glasgow brigade developed a fully enclosed six-wheeled vehicle that looked very much like a bus. Identified as the "New World Body" or an "all-weather pump," it took about two years before firefighters seriously considered it for routine service. In fact, many early versions of fully enclosed vehicles were not given the opportunity to be the primary piece of equipment at an alarm. Rather, these vehicles served as auxiliary equipment.

Although Mack's first enclosed cab was a good five years away, British designers tackled the safety cab with zeal. It didn't hurt their enthusiasm that the new vehicles were quite attractive. Combining the new streamlined designs of automobiles with a concern for safety produced some remarkable fire-fighting rigs.

Early European pioneers of this new movement were the Dennis Brothers and Leyland. One version by Dennis was a body placed on a forward-control, low-loading chassis that provided enclosed seating for the entire crew.

By 1937, a large percentage of fire trucks were equipped with closed cabs, but Mack still offered open cabs as well. This 1937 Mack 75, a 750-gpm [2,838.8l] pumper, displays the flowing lines and bullet headlamps typical of the streamline era.

Indeed, many of these fire engines were set very low to the ground to provide a low center of gravity and stability on the road. Leyland delivered the Cub FK9, which featured an unusual notchback design, to the town of Hinckley, England, in 1940. Another excellent example of Leyland's pre–World War II work was the SFKT2. It was similar to a rounded beetle-shaped delivery van and was shipped to the town of Croydon, England.

Merryweather produced a completely enclosed rig for Edinburgh firefighters, with its pumps just behind the driver's seat, the suction inlet at the rear of the body, and outlets on either side.

These new versions required their crews to alter their routines considerably. Closed cabs provided great locker space to store equipment, but they also meant rearranging the other equipment as well. Pumps, control panels, and ladders were now stored differently. Firefighters were required to undergo extensive training to locate these items without delay. This difficulty was compounded by the fact that few European rigs were standardized, given the low number of fire engines sold.

On the other side of the Atlantic Ocean, Seagrave would emerge as the leader in streamlined closed-cab pumpers. By the late 1930s, it produced a stunning series of fire engines that probably did more than any other vehicle to make closed cabs acceptable.

In 1938, Seagrave delivered a beautiful streamlined 750-gpm [2,838.8l] pumper with a waterfall grille and fully enclosed cab to the fire department in Wakefield, Massachusetts. It weighed 12,200 pounds [5,538.8kg] and cost $9,500. Although expensive, the pumper saw service for twenty-two years. Wakefield was so happy with the rig that it copied the Seagrave style in 1941 and placed a new body on a Dodge chassis to complement the original Seagrave.

In 1939, the Cleveland Fire Department took delivery of a four-door closed-cab pumper that seated eight firefighters, with the driver and engineer sharing the bench front seat.

Falling in line behind Seagrave in styling and engineering were American LaFrance's 600-gallon [2,271l] Protector pumper, Mack's early B series, and Pirsch & Sons' 1936 enclosed-cab model.

In addition to these makers, several hybrids emerged on the market. General, of Detroit, constructed a cab-over-engine design on a 1937 Federal chassis. By 1939 General was using the newly designed Ford cab-over-engine designs to produce several rigs. In 1940, American LaFrance attempted to market the COE designs as well but met with little success. At that point, few buyers preferred the radical new design to the traditional look.

OPPOSITE: A 1936 Mack Junior complemented the Senior line and proved extremely popular with smaller fire agencies during the depression.
LEFT: In 1935, the Rockville Center, New York, fire department took delivery on this American LaFrance 400 Series 1,250-gpm [5,731.3l] pumper with a V12 engine. The 400 Series is considered one of the most beautiful examples of American LaFrance styling.

pump. The rig is also equipped with a 9-inch [22.9cm] searchlight and 9-inch headlights, as well as a solid ash wood extension ladder. It weighs 6,620 pounds [3,005.5kg] and sits on a 140-inch [355.6cm] wheelbase.

The next model in Seagrave's new line was the Standard, which came in two versions, delivering 750 and 1,000 gpm [2,838.8 and 3,785l]. The top of the line was the Metropolite, a 1,300-gpm [4,920.5l] pumper designed for big jobs.

Although the Suburbanite 350 Triple Combination Pumper remained Seagrave's most popular offering, the company continued to make improvements in its line. In 1926, it offered yet another vehicle, the Seagrave Special, to fit between the nimble Suburbanite and the Standard. The Special pumped at 600 gpm [2,271l] and came with a 100-horsepower six-cylinder Hercules engine.

MACK

While Seagrave excited fire departments with its Suburbanite, Mack was determined to reach new heights with its aerial ladders. In 1928, it introduced an engine-dri-ven mechanical hoist for the aerial ladder. Ladders had previously been raised by springs, compressed air, and manual cranking. The new hoist transmitted power from the engine through a vertical shaft that passed directly through the center of the rig's fifth wheel and the aerial ladder's turntable.

Immediately after World War I, the military sold off hundreds of Mack Type AC Bulldogs as war surplus. When the city of Baltimore picked up its ACs at bargain prices, some of the trucks were hitched to ladder wagons that had previously been drawn by horses. In 1922, for example, the Baltimore Fire Department's maintenance shop converted a 1919 Type AC by attaching it to a Holloway horse-drawn ladder/chemical wagon that had been built in 1886. This sort of combination served the city's Ladder Company 24 very well from 1923 until 1952.

Although the Bulldog look remained the company's trademark, Mack did not shy away from experimenting with style changes, even though it did this considerably later than Seagrave had.

Mack debuted its B Series in 1927 and manufactured more than 15,000 of the machines by the end of 1941. Easily

identified by their side hood louvers and doors, B models came in various sizes, such as the Type 75, powered by a 110-horsepower engine and equipped with a 750-gpm [2,838.8l] pump.

San Francisco's fire department had a fondness for the Type 15 model AP rigs, purchasing two in 1928 and 1929. The AP version had a chain drive, four-wheel brakes, and an electric starter. It was powered by a 150-horsepower engine and carried a 1,000-gpm [3,785l] pump. The standard AP rigs were popular with many departments, but some departments got creative about customizing Mack products. The department in Ross, California, transformed a Mack AL chassis originally designed for a bus into a fire engine. Its 1928 Type 90 model came equipped with the Byron-Jackson 1,000-gpm [3,785l] pump and a 90-gallon [340.7l] water tank.

PIRSCH

Compared with Seagrave and Mack, Peter Pirsch & Sons was rather slow out of the gate with styling and technical innovations. It wasn't until 1926 that the company began building fire engines on its own chassis, but it did produce some fine machines by joining commercial chassis with its own elaborate apparatus.

In the early 1920s, Pirsch built a flashy combination hose and chemical car on a Packard chassis, in accordance with a customer's specifications; and in 1920 Pirsch worked a similar transformation on a rather dowdy four-cylinder Oldsmobile commercial chassis. The company also used chassis from Rambler (later to become Nash), as well as the obscure Atterbury. For many years, the fire department in Aberdeen, Washington, used a 1913 Atterbury-Pirsch city service truck, which featured a chain drive, hard rubber tires, and a chemical tank. The headlights were Dietz "King" oil lanterns.

Pirsch also never built its own engine, preferring to use almost exclusively the Waukesha six-cylinder fire service models. These heavy-duty, low-speed, high-torque engines ranged from 525 to 1,090 cubic inches [3,200 to 6,650cc], with horsepower ranging from 226 to 318.

Pirsch's reputation received its biggest boost on April 14, 1931, when a tunnel in Chicago collapsed. The company

This 1922 Pirsch city service ladder truck was manufactured on an REO chassis and purchased by the Wilson, North Carolina, fire department.

WATER TOWERS

As American cities grew taller, firefighters were faced with the new problem of battling blazes in buildings that reached ten stories. Ground-based water treatment of such fires was largely ineffective, because the stream of water often failed to reach the source of the conflagration. Firefighters first attacked the problem by running hose lines up several stories along their ladders. But it was a risky business, particularly if rescues were involved.

In 1869, a Chicago inventor, known only as Mr. Skinner, produced the first patented "hose elevator," which was used in the great Chicago fire of 1871. The hose elevator reached up to 40 feet [12.2m] high and sucked water out of a bucket-type device that was elevated with the hose. It was crude and its effectiveness was questionable, but the Chicago Fire Department liked the device enough that it used two of them for about two years.

The first successful invention for shooting water horizontally into a building's upper floors was developed by Albert and Abner Greenleaf and John B. Logan in 1876. Based in Baltimore, they built a water tower consisting of three sections. The base was mounted on the floor of the wagon. The second section was a piece of straight pipe connected to the base. The last piece—a 1½-inch [3.8cm] extension pipe—was equipped with a nozzle tip.

A cable braced the main straight pipe, and it was raised with a hand crank.

This 50-foot [15.2m] tower was tested by the New York Fire Department in 1879, and it performed very well. The fire department purchased the tower for $4,000, then purchased a second one in 1882. Boston also purchased one before Logan and the Greenleafs sold their rights to the Fire Extinguisher Manufacturing Company of Chicago.

The new owners, however, found themselves in a quandary almost immediately. In large part, it was thanks to Kansas City fire chief George C. Hale, who also served as president of the Kansas City Fire Supply Company, that their water tower was quickly outdated. Hale invented a water tower that stood 75 feet [22.9m] high and operated on a combination chemical-hydraulic lifting system.

This system used water pressure to force soda and acid from two tanks into two cylinders, where they combined. The gas released by the soda-acid reaction in the cylinders lifted the tower to its full height. It was a reliable and effective system, and thirty-eight of the water towers were constructed between 1886 and 1892.

Hale's invention spurred the Fire Extinguisher Manufacturing Company to compete in earnest. It developed a tower that was placed on a turntable to operate either at an angle or vertically. It also featured a new nozzle. Called the Champion, it shared the same name as the company's popular chemical engines.

The company sold its first water tower, a 65-footer [19.8m], to the Detroit Fire Department in 1893 and it went on to service dozens of other fire departments for more than three decades.

Along with the development of water towers came new technology in aerials. Seagrave produced a 75-foot ladder [22.9m] that was installed on its first aerial truck and shipped to the District of Columbia in 1902.

Other ladder makers developed their own technology with a great degree of success. Skinner's ladders reached up to 100 feet [30.5m], while Hayes developed a special crank riser for its aerials. Babcock, a leading manufacturer of fire-fighting equipment, produced a ladder raised by vertical worm screws on either side of the turntable base.

By 1917, American LaFrance had began focusing on developing an 85-foot [25.9m] self-erecting ladder using spring counterweights, replacing the laborious poles and ropes that firefighters used to raise a ladder. The invention saved crucial time and labor in raising ladders at alarms.

HALE WATER-TOWER.

had just produced the first practical engine designed to draw or blow smoke out of buildings and tunnels, blow out grass fires, and remove poisonous fumes from enclosed areas. The idea for the engine was proposed by Minneapolis fire chief Charles W. Ringer, and it later came to be identified by the fire-fighting industry as the Pirsch-Ringer smoke ejector. With sixteen men trapped in the collapsed tunnel, the Chicago Fire Department requested the smoke ejector. Untested, with its paint barely dry, the new truck—under police escort—reached Chicago from the Pirsch plant 60 miles [96km] away in eighty-eight minutes, and was used immediately. It saved the lives of all sixteen men.

AHRENS-FOX

The years between the wars marked the most successful period for Ahrens-Fox, as it continued to produce some of the most massive examples of fire-fighting equipment ever man-

ufactured. But, perhaps in response to Seagrave's Suburbanite, Ahrens-Fox also developed a modest "quad," the Skirmisher, in its quest to enter the lower-priced market. The most common fire engine of the day was the "triple," but the quad, with pump, hose, booster tank, and ground ladder, was something special.

Ahrens-Fox appliances were extremely popular with the city of Detroit, which purchased twenty-four Model J 750-gpm [2,838.8l] piston pumpers in 1927. These models were equipped with a distinctive windshield with a leather-made frame mounted on the cowl. Dr. Peter Molloy, director of the Hall of Flame Museum in Phoenix, Arizona, notes that these windshields were not seen outside of Detroit. "I suspect the fire commissioner's brother-in-law probably had some deal with the fire department to make these and install them," Molloy observes wryly.

Ahrens-Fox debuted the Skirmisher in 1929, equipped with a modest 500-gpm [1,892.5l] pump. Although these lit-

This 1930 Ahrens-Fox Skirmisher was delivered to the town of Haledon, New Jersey.

tle beauties proved popular, Ahrens-Fox made a more significant contribution to fire fighting with two new ladder trucks, the N-S-444 and the H-44. These trucks were each powered by six-cylinder engines and carried 238 feet [72.5m] of ladder, including three roof ladders with folding hooks, three wall ladders, and three extension ladders. The company used its "Double Bank" method to store the ladders in a nesting position. They were set on steel guides and held in position by locking clamps at front and rear. All models were equipped with four-wheel brakes and a booster auxiliary brake. Optional equipment included a chemical tank, a booster pump, or an auxiliary tank.

Ahrens-Fox was proud of its offerings, and with good reason. During the 1920s and 1930s, the company stood for majestic excellence, with its piston pumper weighing 13,700 pounds [6,219.8kg] and spanning 25 feet [7.6m].

But like many manufacturers of expensive vehicles, Ahrens-Fox was done in by the Great Depression. In 1938, it followed such legends of luxury as Duesenberg, Cord, and Auburn in declaring bankruptcy. It reemerged a little the worse for wear but managed to limp along into the 1950s.

THE V12 ENGINE

As independent automakers fell victim to the Great Depression, builders of luxury cars didn't appear to get the message that ostentatious machines reeking of money were no longer in good taste. Nevertheless, if one could afford it, the thought of owning a multicylinder car (a car, that is, with more than eight cylinders) was very attractive. It was hard to deny the appeal of a twelve- or sixteen-cylinder engine, with its earthy growl, capable of speeds up to 100 miles per hour [160kph]. Gasoline mileage wasn't great, but that hardly mattered to anyone who could afford up to $10,000 for some of the finest examples of luxury motoring ever produced.

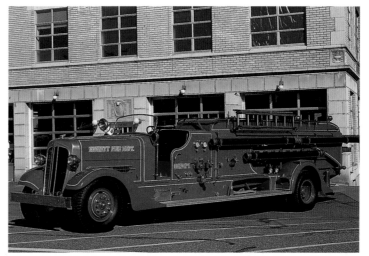

LEFT: The Everett, Washington, fire department was the proud owner of this 1937 Ahrens-Fox 750-gpm [2,838.8l] pumper, built without the trademark front-mounted pump.

BELOW: This 1928 Ahrens-Fox 750-gpm [2,838.8l] pumper is more typical of the artistry of the maker's trucks, with the elaborate pumping system mounted up front. Although somewhat archaic compared with rotary pumps, fire departments nonetheless prized these beauties for their looks and mystique.

Cadillac, Auburn, and Pierce-Arrow had considerable success with multicylinder cars, and it was only a matter of time before truck makers would follow. In 1931, American LaFrance introduced its V12.

The company designed and produced its V12 in secrecy. It is difficult to imagine now why such an engine would be necessary. Most of these trucks were usually driven just a few blocks, or perhaps a few miles, down the street. But fire engine builders reasoned that more power was needed to haul heavier equipment to a blaze, and when it comes to fighting fires, faster is definitely better.

American LaFrance's first V12 offering performed poorly in early demonstrations, but it sparked a new trend among its competitors. Seagrave had been developing a V12 since the early 1920s, yet still couldn't beat American LaFrance to the market. Its V12 version debuted in 1932. The American LaFrance version generated only 249 horsepower and required 7 gallons [26.5l] of oil to lubricate. It had a displacement of 754 cubic inches [46m³] with a 4-by-5 bore and stroke.

Seagrave, however, developed a much stronger multicylinder engine. Styled after the Pierce-Arrow, the Seagrave V12 had a displacement of 906 cubic inches [5,530cc] with Stromberg DDR-5 dual-thrown downdraft carburetors. Later versions came equipped with dual Zenith carburetors. The valves could be replaced without removing the head and ports, because they were easily accessible underneath the spark plugs. This was a boon to mechanics: carbon buildup on valves was common because of the unstable gasoline quality of the era, and frequent repairs were necessary. Seagrave offered its V12, called the E-66 (E for engine and 66 for the two rows of six cylinders each), in two versions, generating either 160 or 185 horsepower.

THE METROPOLITAN

Perhaps more significant than American La France's V12 was its Series 400 Metropolitan.

The company's first Metropolitan debuted in 1926 as the Series 100 and was very attractive and functional. The

Series 100 was followed in 1929 with the Series 200, known as the Master, then the Series 300 in 1933, the 400 in 1935, and the 500 in 1938.

The Series 400 Metropolitan was American LaFrance's crowning achievement. With its massive pumping capacity and fenders trimmed in gold leaf like the most outrageous luxury cars of the day, it was the perfect marriage of style and technology.

The company manufactured about 150 Senior Metropolitans, many of them triple combination pumpers. Others were constructed as hose wagons, quad combinations, and ladder trucks.

By the mid-1930s, American LaFrance had solved some of its early problems with the V12, and it began fitting them into the Metropolitans without mufflers. Firefighters were as thrilled by the noise as they were by the power of these monstrous vehicles. Firefighters also liked the fact that the pump was placed astern of the power plant and directly in front of the cab. The truck came on a 180-inch [457.2cm] wheelbase with 24-inch [61cm] wheels. The rotary-gear or centrifugal pumps were available in 1,000-, 1,250-, or 1,500-gpm [3,785, 4,731.5, or 5,677.5l] versions.

A year before the debut of the Senior Metropolitan, American LaFrance offered its Junior line. It featured a straight-eight Lycoming engine built by Auburn, with the pump more conventionally placed behind the cab. These rigs were designated according to their pumping capacity. A Scout had a capacity of 500 gpm [1,892l], the Protector 600 gpm [2,271l], and the Invader 750 gpm [2,838.8l].

CLOSED CABS

Although firefighters were thrilled by the introduction of the powerful V12 engine and by the new attention paid to aesthetic considerations, there were some innovations that just didn't sit well with them.

The old-timers saw the twentieth century do away with their beloved horses and their perfectly capable steam engines. Springs and engines were now doing some of the work that had previously been done by sheer muscle power, and electric starters and four-wheel brakes had begun to diminish the macho appeal of operating the machines. But the one innovation that firefighters found hardest to accept was the closed cab.

Although Mack would receive much of the credit (and blame) for introducing the closed-cab fire engine in 1935, it was not the first to bring such a design to market. In 1931,

While Mack received most of the credit for introducing the closed-cab fire engine, this 1928 Pirsch 600-gpm [2,271l] pumper helped pave the way, although it did little to change firefighters' minds.

This 1935 American-LaFrance Series 400 Metropolitan was still serving Clarksdale, Mississippi, in 1953. Note the unusual "squirrel tail" preconnected hard suction hose.

This 1929 Seagrave 500-gpm [1,892.5] pumper is owned by the Leesburg, Virginia, volunteer fire department.

A closed-cab 1939 Mack 80 750-gpm [2,838.8] pumper belonging to the Clinton, Massachusetts, fire department.

Dennis constructed a fully enclosed pumper for the Edinburgh Fire Brigade in England. And in 1928, seven years before Mack's model debuted, Pirsch delivered the first fire truck with a fully closed cab. It was a 600-gpm [2,271l] pumper purchased by Monroe, Wisconsin.

But Mack's 1935 outing started a trend that wouldn't quit, despite negative reviews from the rough-and-tumble fire-fighting community. These men, after all, prided themselves on their disregard for danger and discomfort; a closed cab seemed a luxury for milquetoasts, not firemen. Firefighters wouldn't fully embrace the closed cab until after World War II, but no one could deny that it had obvious advantages.

Mack produced its fire sedan at the suggestion of Charlotte, North Carolina, fire chief Hendrix Palmer, who believed that firefighters should respond to alarms in comfort and safety.

The Mack Type 19 B series could seat ten firefighters and accompanying equipment inside, with the hard suction hoses remaining mounted outside the vehicle. Besides feeling

like sissies hiding inside the cab, firefighters also felt that the new machine just didn't look like a fire engine.

In 1936, Seagrave offered its Canopy Cab or Safety Sedan. Some of Seagrave's early efforts were enclosed box-shaped versions built of wood and sheet metal for the Detroit Fire Department. But as these units were being put together, the company recognized that only reinforced steel would work for a fully enclosed fire truck.

These new versions could seat seven men, with two separate compartments for 750 feet [228.6m] of hose each and a 100-gallon [378.5l] water tank.

In 1936, the fire department in Bar Harbor, Maine, took delivery of its first Canopy Cab; it resembled a dual cab pickup truck, with about half the firefighters seated in the bed.

The improved safety of closed-cab fire engines was demonstrated dramatically in 1936, when an Ahrens-Fox hose truck and a closed-cab Seagrave collided in Detroit while responding to an alarm. The hose truck struck the sedan broadside, bending the frame 7 inches [17.8cm]. Firefighters in the Seagrave were not hurt, but the men in the

OPPOSITE PAGE: A New York City firefighter levels a stationary hose at a blaze at the Moore Brothers lumberyard at 24th Street and 11th Avenue.

BELOW: This 1923 Boyer combination was built on a Service Motor Truck Company (Wabash, Indiana) chassis. The chemical tanks and body were constructed by Boyer at the Logansport, Indiana, plant.

ABOVE: The brilliantly polished bell and spotlight of a vintage fire engine.

Ahrens-Fox sustained serious injuries. The results made an impression on Detroit city officials, who authorized the purchase of nine sedan-style pumpers in 1937 and 1938.

OTHER MANUFACTURERS

The economic boom of the 1920s brought a slew of new fire equipment manufacturers, most of whom were just as quickly dispatched by the Great Depression in the 1930s.

The Buffalo Fire Extinguishing Manufacturing Company lasted longer than many of its contemporaries, hanging on until 1948. Founded in Buffalo, New York, in 1920, the company sold equipment primarily in the East, where it concentrated on helping municipalities switch from horse-drawn fire equipment to motorized units. It specialized in using other commercial chassis, most notably the Larrabee, to mount its fire engine bodies. It also used Ford Model T and Model A chassis.

Buffalo began building its own chassis in the early 1930s and in 1939 introduced its streamlined look with long, sleek hoods, fully enclosed cabs, and a distinctive style.

The Sanford Fire Apparatus Company didn't fare as well as Buffalo and didn't last nearly as long. Founded in 1908, it built its own trucks on its own chassis until 1925. It also used other manufacturers' chassis and built a series of trucks to buyers' specifications. Sanford managed to stay in business through World War II as one of the last businesses to convert Model T chassis to fire-fighting uses.

Perhaps its most significant accomplishment came in the mid-1920s when it developed the 528 pumper nicknamed the Cub. The 500-gpm [1,892.5l] pumper was meant to compete directly with Seagrave's Suburbanite in serving small towns and cities wishing to convert to motorized apparatus on a tight budget.

Of the fire engine manufacturers that were founded during the years between the wars, there was one that survived the tumultuous economy of the time and continues to thrive today. Ward LaFrance emerged from the Great Depression to be a leader in the industry, despite the fact that in some fire-fighting quarters its name lives in infamy. For Ward LaFrance brought lime-yellow paint, known to firefighters as "slime lime," to fire engines (see p. 92). The company insisted that the color is more visible at night than red. Nevertheless, firefighters through the years have steadfastly persisted in maintaining that red with a bold white stripe is more visible under any conditions than any green.

Not to be confused with American LaFrance, although both companies were founded in Elmira, New York, Ward

RIGHT: Gauges for monitoring water and air pressure.
FAR RIGHT: The Buffalo Fire Appliance Corporation was a small builder of firefighting apparatus in the 1930s. Its products, all decorated with this elegant porcelain badge, were largely confined to the East Coast.

LaFrance focused on building custom pumpers during the 1930s. During the postwar era, it tended to build larger rigs.

During this period, there were also a number of smaller, more obscure ventures, which were nonetheless important to fire-fighting services.

The Moreland Truck Company of Burbank, California, sold several brush trucks to the Los Angeles County Fire Department in 1930. Most of these vehicles were equipped with a 650-gallon [2,460.3l] water tank that feeds to a small pump under the driver's seat. In 1927, Moreland sent a similar version to the Mount Shasta, California, fire department. It came equipped with a six-cylinder flathead Continental engine, four-speed transmission, and four-wheel hydraulic brakes. It has been restored and is now owned by an organization called Fire Fighters for Christ International.

The Kissel Motor Car Company of Hartford, Wisconsin, known primarily for manufacturing sporty cars, built a fire truck for its hometown in 1920. It converted a 1900 Seagrave horse-drawn ladder wagon with a 60-foot [18.3m] extension ladder weighing more than 600 pounds [272.4kg] and requiring a crew of six firefighters to operate.

The Brockway Truck Company of Cortland, New York, constructed a handful of fire trucks, although it con-

fined itself to building chassis after about 1920. In 1921, American LaFrance used a light Brockway "Torpedo" chassis to build a small chemical truck with three chemical tanks and two booster hoses.

Another unusual offering available during the 1920s and 1930s was apparatus fitted on REO Speedwagons. REO was founded by inventor Ransom Eli Olds, who in 1899 also founded the Olds Motor Works, which later became Oldsmobile. In 1930, REO built a triple combination pumper for the Bellmond, Iowa, fire department, which purchased the machine on a U.S. Treasury bond. Now in the care of firefighters in Rancho Cucamonga, California, the pumper is powered by a Gold Crown 268-cubic-inch [1,600cc], 47-horsepower engine. It is equipped with a pair of 37-gallon [140l] tanks, a 24-foot [7.3m] truss ladder, and a 14-foot [4.3m] roof ladder. It also has a 500-gpm [1,892.5l] Hale rotary gear-driven pump. It served Bellmond faithfully for thirty-two years.

In 1948, the county records office in Bellmond caught fire, and the newer rigs were too big to fit into a narrow alley near the burning building. Firefighters called for the REO to squeeze in to help transfer water and supplies to other engines. It was the last time the machine saw primary service. It was retired in 1962.

BELOW: A combination truck, this rare 1931 REO Speedwagon/Maxim 250-gpm [1,946.3] pumper primarily served small towns in the East.

FOLLOWING PAGE: This 1934 American LaFrance 200 Series featured a 750-gpm [2,838.8l], rotary gear pump and a V12 engine. It was delivered to the Cumberland, Maryland, fire department.

TOP: Mack sales surged in the mid-1950s with the introduction of pumpers such as this 1956 open-cab model sold to the Anna State Hospital, in Anna, Illinois.
BOTTOM: A 1952 GMC closed-cab fire engine. Note the civil defense emblem on the door of this Millington Fire Department pumper.

CHAPTER THREE

1941 / 1960

WHEN THE UNITED STATES ENTERED WORLD WAR II, NEW COMMERCIAL AND LIGHT-DUTY TRUCK REGISTRATIONS PLUMMETED AS TRUCK MAKERS GEARED UP FOR THE WAR EFFORT.

In 1942, new truck registrations amounted to just 77,422, dropping dramatically from 640,697 the previous year. The year 1943 saw a significant decline as well, with only 62,469 new trucks registered in the country.

Like commercial truck makers, builders of fire apparatus also pitched in to help America win the war. Major builders like Seagrave and Mack continued constructing fire engines during the war years because fire-fighting equipment was considered essential. But many of these engines were shipped overseas between 1942 and 1945 and remained there to see service for more than three decades.

By the early 1940s, cities were changing over to aluminum aerials, although some fire departments, such as New York City's, clung stubbornly to their wood aerials. In 1941, Seagrave delivered seven 75-foot [22.9m] wood aerials to New York.

New York may have had a point. Although wood ladders, of course, could burn, early aluminum aerials had a ten-dency to lose their strength and warp more, because of riveted construction; aluminum welding had yet to be perfected.

Because fire engine makers were now working for the military, civilian fire departments had to make do with their Depression-era apparatus. Seagrave, however, managed to get in one more significant makeover before converting to wartime production. The manufacturer dropped the old-style grille that had debuted in 1935 and began using a more rounded front that had been on many of its smaller trucks since 1936. In addition, a new raked windshield was introduced that would become a mainstay of Seagrave styling.

Mack also came out with a new line, the rugged L Series truck; over the next seventeen years, Mack delivered 33,000 thousand of the machines to fire departments. Considered the king of the hill by commercial users as well as firefighters, the L Series remains the best example of Mack's advanced engineering.

PREVIOUS PAGE:
New York City firefighters battle a five-alarm blaze in a clothing store on Manhattan's Lower East Side in 1963. Twelve firefighters and one civilian woman were overcome by smoke.

TOP RIGHT: It may look a little ungainly, and it's not painted traditional red, but this 1941 closed-cab Mack elicits a lot of admiration from today's enthusiasts.

BOTTOM RIGHT: Another example of a closed-cab Seagrave, this one a 1947 Model 80 750-gpm [2,838.8l] pumper.

These vehicles were powered by a large 707A or 707B dual-ignition gasoline engine that provided excellent pumping performance. Most of these trucks came with a four-speed transmission, and they were usually fitted with either 750-gpm [2,838.8l] or 1,250-gpm [4,731.3l] centrifugal pumps. Those delivered to some larger cities, such as Minneapolis, carried a Hall-Scott engine with a massive 2,000-gpm [7,570l] pumper.

By the end of the war, builders were eager to satisfy the huge demand for new fire engines. For five long years, cities and smaller burgs throughout the United States had had to maintain their old rigs with increasing ingenuity as parts became more scarce. Some towns brought out their old horse-drawn steamers and found ways to attach them to commercial trucks or to their aging fire engines.

Many truck builders didn't get into the full swing of postwar production until the 1948 model year, but 1946 proved to be a good year for production nonetheless. New

truck registrations in 1946 rose 17 percent, with 625,259 new trucks on the road, bringing the total number of trucks in the country to 5,749,643. Chevrolet led the way with more than 171,000 new trucks manufactured, and Ford came in second with nearly 132,000 new rigs.

New truck registrations climbed another 15 percent in 1947, and new registrations broke the 1 million mark for the first time ever, with 1.035 million trucks rolling out of factory doors.

To say that it was a seller's market during these heady years would be an understatement. There was a tremendous backlog, with cities like Chicago, Baltimore, and Los Angeles replacing virtually their entire fleets.

As the war began to wind down, the city of Los Angeles purchased eighteen triple combinations from Peter Pirsch & Sons in 1945. These triples were equipped with sturdy Hall-Scott engines and four-speed transmissions. In the same year, the department also purchased an American

American LaFrance was the front-runner in cab-forward fire engine design after World War II. Fire departments, particularly large agencies like New York City's, clamored for these modern-looking behemoths. This 1949 American LaFrance 700 Series quad combination was purchased by the Findlay, Ohio, fire department.

9062-R

WAR YEARS

As early as 1937, the British government began planning for the possibility of war with Germany. Recognizing that in the event of war, attack by German airplanes was probable, the government issued a memorandum announcing that 200,000 auxiliary firefighters were needed to train for anticipated emergencies.

Although there had been many technological advances since the previous war, England inexplicably had a poor and disorganized fire service plan. A little more than 16,000 men were available in hundreds of fire brigades, but only one quarter of them were trained, experienced firefighters. Equipment was antiquated, and in some rural areas, brigade uniforms were nonexistent.

Fire brigades around the country were initially enthusiastic about the government's commitment to modernizing them with state-of-the-art equipment. They were disappointed when, instead of the latest engines, they received trailer pumps or self-contained pumping units mounted on lorries. They were especially disgusted when they were issued miniature wheelbarrow pumps, equipped with a tiny centrifugal pump, driven by a single-cylinder gasoline engine, though by the end of the war the little devices had proven themselves many times over.

In addition, Britain's traditional arrogance in ignoring the standardization of mechanical equipment that was common throughout other European countries finally exacted a toll. Hoses, couplers, nozzles, and hydrants didn't match from region to region, and equipment could not easily be shared.

With these drawbacks, the Auxiliary Fire Service (AFS) was formed. But it wasn't until the Munich Crisis of 1938 (when Germany invaded Czechoslovakia) that the AFS neared its goal of becoming fully organized with 100,000 men ready for wartime emergencies. The Munich Crisis did prompt the Home Office to allocate 1 million pounds to fund new equipment.

When England declared war against Germany in September 1939, its citizens fully expected to be hit by

RIGHT: Unlike their American counterparts, European fire departments, such as this pre–World War II Czech fire squad, put an emphasis on safety by placing their personnel inside the fire engine.
OPPOSITE PAGE: Firefighters struggle to beat back flames shooting from buildings along Queen Victoria Street in London during the German Blitz in 1941. The international headquarters of the Salvation Army is at right. Firefighters were well prepared, but hundreds of fires started simultaneously by intense bombings still devastated the city.

heavy air attacks from the dreaded Luftwaffe. But the attacks failed to materialize during the first year of war, and those precious weeks and months gave firefighters an opportunity to conduct further intense training and gather necessary equipment.

The training paid off. In the summer of 1940, the German Blitzkrieg struck. Croydon Airport, the West India Docks, and the towns of Woolwich and Eltham were bombed. Fires blazed, but the AFS responded remarkably well despite being undermanned at the hoses. To make up the shortage of personnel, the government began conscripting men and women into the AFS.

On September 5, 1940, 600 German aircraft dropped incendiary devices on London. More than a thousand fires raged through the night. For nearly two months, the Luftwaffe blitzed London every night. In November, the German attackers struck Coventry, Liverpool, Sheffield, and Birmingham.

Despite heroic efforts, the AFS was faced with some severe problems. Shipyards and docks had a water supply close by, but other areas hit by bombers were left to the mercy of the flames when water mains were ruptured. It also appeared the Germans kept a close eye on the tides in the River Thames. When the tide was low, bombs dropped with sickening regularity. On December 29, 1940, 1,500 fires were ignited by approximately 100,000 bombs, and firefighters on the bridges of London stood by helplessly as the blazes swept out of control. A valuable lesson was learned when a string of Ford-Sulzer trailer pumps were later placed on bridges over the Thames where they could suck up water regardless of how low the tide was.

There were several pump suppliers that kept firefighters well equipped during England's war years. Apex, Beresford, Coventry-Climax, Dennis Brothers, Forest Protection, Gwyne, Harland, Pyrene, Sigmund, Sulzer, and Worthington-Simpson all provided trailer pumps that proved vital to controlling blazes.

Pumps came in three sizes: light, medium, and large. The light trailer pump carried a 140- to 175-gallon [529.9l to 662.4l] tank, and pumped water with a two-stage centrifugal pump powered by either a two- or four-cylinder gasoline engine. It was mounted on a two-wheel trailer and could be towed by a car. The medium trailer pump had a four-cylinder, 12-horsepower engine powering a single-stage centrifugal pump with a 230- to 320-gallon [870.6l to 1,211.2l] tank. The larger trailer pump had a maximum

tank capacity of 500 gallons [1,892.5l], with either a four- or eight-cylinder engine to power a single or two-stage centrifugal pump. Many of these trailer pumps were towed by commandeered taxis or fire engines fashioned from chopped cars or trucks.

In August 1941, the National Fire Service was organized in an effort to coordinate operations and communications better. The country was divided into thirty-three fire areas over eleven regions. Fire brigades were consolidated into a single organization for each fire area.

By 1945, London firefighters had responded to more than 50,000 alarms. The London Region Fire Service employed 42,000 men and 10,000 vehicles during the height of its service.

The Germans were much better prepared for wartime fire service. They developed a series of light,

medium, and heavy pumpers, turntable-ladders, foam trucks, and tank pumpers ranging from 1^1/$_2$ tons to 4^1/$_2$ tons [1.4t to 4.1t].

Daimler-Benz, Klockner-Humbolt-Duetz, and Opel supplied chassis. Fischer, Flader, Hoenig, Magirus, Mayer-Hagen, Metz, Koebe, and Rosenbauer provided bodies and various equipment.

In 1941, for example, Mercedes-Benz supplied the Luftwaffe with several fully enclosed Magirus-bodied cabs. These big trucks provided ladders on top of the vehicle, but virtually all other equipment was stowed inside a dozen or so compartments.

Opel developed the four-wheel drive Opel-Blitz on a short wheelbase around 1943. Another Opel-Blitz, introduced in 1944, was a four-wheel drive version with a Magirus tanker body on a 3-ton [2.7t] chassis.

One of the most important lessons that the Germans learned during the war was the need to have equipment capable of negotiating bombed-out streets. The German Fire Service discovered that two-wheel-drive fire apparatus was ineffective in war zones. Following the war, the Federal Republic's Department of Civil Defense authorized the manufacture of all-terrain fire engines. Mercedes' tactical vehicle, called the "Unimog," was fitted as a standard fire engine with a 350-gallon [1,324.8kg] water tank and 350-gpm [1,324.8l] pump. It was identified as the Mercedes/Metz All-Terrain Fire Engine. The truck also was equipped with many tools, fittings, and hoses and towed a trailer equipped with a foam tank for use at electrical and oil fires.

In the early 1960s, the Phoenix, Arizona, fire department purchased about a half dozen of these compact vehi-

This Pirsch was one of many Model 20G 750-gpm [2,838.8] pumpers supplied to the U.S. Army between 1941 and 1943. Note the open seat and split windshield. Also, this model was early enough that it still did not receive the blackout treatment on its chrome.

cles for fighting brushfires. But the weight of the tanks on these trucks was poorly distributed, and the machines tended to tip over on steep hills. They quickly became unpopular, but the department continues to use a few of them today.

The wartime experiences of American firefighters were nothing compared with those of their British and German colleagues. Nevertheless, Americans also had to improvise during wartime.

In New York City, in the weeks following the December 7, 1941, bombing of Pearl Harbor, firefighters were trained to identify bombs and poisonous gas and disposal methods. Much equipment, such as trailers to store explosive devices, was constructed of steel and could be towed by any vehicle that a firefighter could commandeer. Other trailers carried up to 500 feet [152.4m] of hose, a 16-foot [4.9m] ladder, a first-aid kit, and other small pieces of equipment needed for a variety of emergencies.

Like the automotive industry, fire engine makers saw their output dwindle from a peak of about 1,500 new fire engines manufactured in 1928 to about 800 in 1938. Cities and counties scaled back their purchasing budgets, many of them deciding it was more economical to repair old fire engines rather than investing in an expensive alternative.

U.S. truck registrations were very low between 1937 and 1940. New truck registrations in 1938 dropped by 252,900 compared with the previous year. Not since the depths of the Great Depression had so few trucks made it to the road.

But fire-fighting vehicle companies still reaped some benefits from wartime production. Fire-fighting equipment was considered essential during the war. Cities, however, had to prove that a new fire engine was necessary for the community before they could get approval for the purchase. Municipalities then had to content themselves with

Unlike the Pirsch on the previous page, this 1942 Buffalo 500-gpm [1,892.5l] pumper with a three-man cab received the full blackout treatment because of World War II restrictions.

new trucks without chrome plating or burnished copper parts, which were deemed strategic metal, and could be used only for military purposes. And since sirens were generally used to signal an air attack, many such devices on fire engines were banned. Firefighters, not without some pride, resorted to old-fashioned bells and exhaust whistles to alert the local populace.

The government also had the right to seize city-owned fire engines for its own purposes, no matter how obscure. The Corona, California, fire department purchased a brand-new 1942 E Series Type 75 Mack (sans chrome and burnished copper) equipped with a Thermodyne 155-horsepower dual-ignition 510-cubic-inch [3,110cc] engine and four-speed transmission. It also featured a 750-gpm [2,838.8l] two-stage Hale pump. The military liked what it saw and grabbed the engine for purposes that were never made clear to Corona city officials. But they returned it without so much as a scratch on August 24, 1942, and it

went on to see more than three decades of service. The pumper continues to see service today, when it is trotted out for parades and other civic events.

Seagrave manufactured a fleet of pumpers for the U.S. Navy during the war. In 1944, twenty pumpers were built that were equipped with a two-stage bronze 750-gpm [2,838.8l] pump. Five of the pumpers were shipped to Pearl Harbor.

One 1944 pumper, now in the hands of Alan Gilliam of Riverside, California, is an E-66 model powered by a 461-cubic-inch [2,110cc] V12 with a rating of 202 horsepower at 3,700 rpm. Gilliam's Seagrave was first delivered to a naval base at Spring Lake, Oregon. It was later purchased as war surplus by the city of Independence, California. Ten years later it was sent to the Cabazon, California, fire department. It was retired in 1972 and spent most of its time in a Riverside rental yard gathering dirt and rust until Gilliam rescued it in 1982. It's now fully restored.

London firefighters mop up after a German bombing attack left much of this neighborhood in ruins in September 1940.

LaFrance 100-foot [30.5m] aerial powered by a V12 engine. The following year it bought a Seagrave 100-foot [30.5m] aerial also powered by a V12 engine. The Seagrave saw service until 1969.

In late 1945, American LaFrance came out with its radical new Series 700 cab-forward pumper, which set the standard for fire engine design up to the present day. Cab-over-engines and closed-cab designs were still struggling for acceptance in the fire-fighting community. American LaFrance's decision to debut its cab-forward look was a tremendous risk: if the Series 700 had been rejected outright, the company could well have found itself in very serious financial trouble.

The Series 700 was indeed radical but not so far out that firefighters couldn't stand to look at it. In fact, it embodied all the characteristics that firefighters expected in their machines. It was a practical engine that was low and sleek, and it came with either open or closed cab. Either way, it caught the attention of both the firefighter and the public in postwar America. It handled well in tight curves, was shorter than the Series 500, had greater visibility, and had plenty of easily accessible storage space.

American LaFrance delivered its first two cab-forward 700 pumpers to Elkhart, Indiana. They were a pair of closed-cab 1,250-gpm [4.731.3l] models, and they achieved great success. Binghamton, New York, received an 85-foot [25.9m] aerial with a closed cab, and Middletown, New York, was delivered a fleet of new pumpers as well. New York City went for the Series 700 in a big way, ordering twenty pumpers in 1947. True to New York City tradition, all these trucks were equipped with a single length of hard suction hose and one scaling ladder on each side. The pumpers had fixed turret pipes and inlets for the deck pipe. Ten men traveled with each truck: three firefighters sat on the front seat with two more riding in seats on each side of the engine compartment, while three more men rode on the rear step. By June 1947, American LaFrance staked its entire reputation on the 700 Series. It dropped the rest of its line and built 700s exclusively.

Seagrave went into large-scale production and focused its energies on its canopy-cab models, which looked striking with their new V-shaped raked windshield. This design carried Seagrave through the mid-1950s.

The long-suffering Ahrens-Fox continued to limp along after its reorganization in 1938. By 1946, it had abandoned its old plant on Colerian Avenue in Cincinnati and moved to the suburb of Norwood on Beech Street.

The company still manufactured its renowned piston pumper, but other makers' centrifugal pumps were beginning to take a lot of wind out of its sails. Production fell off dramatically as cost-conscious fire departments saw that centrifugal pump designs were simpler, cheaper, and more dependable than the piston pump. During the postwar years, Ahrens-Fox eventually fell in line with its competitors and began building a centrifugal pumper. Meanwhile, its one 1,000-gpm [3,785l] model HT piston pumper—virtually unchanged since 1936—continued to be powered by a Hercules engine.

Not to be outdone by Seagrave, Mack, and American LaFrance, the Maxim Motor Co. came out with a new line of stunning pumpers restyled from top to bottom. It offered city service ladder trucks and quadruple combinations. The new line offered a vertically styled grille; a V-type windshield similar to Seagrave's; open, closed, and canopy cabs; and new pumpers ranging from a modest 750 gpm [2,838.8l] to a massive 1,500 gpm [5,677.5l].

Maxim would build any type of fire engine according to customer specifications. The Shenandoah Heights, Pennsylvania, fire department ordered a 1947 750-gpm [2,838.8l] pumper constructed on an extra-long wheelbase with a four-door cab. The pumper came equipped with an overhead ladder rack and a pair of floodlights mounted on the cab roof. It also offered a very stylish closed-cab 750-gpm [2,838.8l] quad with an enclosed pump panel.

Pirsch & Sons constructed several different types of closed cabs. Its most popular was the two-door cab pumper, but the company offered three other types: the semicab style, the canopy cab, and the four-door sedan. Each cab was built for heavy-duty fire service, with all metal construction.

BELOW: A vintage postwar closed-cab Mack fire engine. **OPPOSITE:** A platform rises high above a fire engine in Mount Pleasant, Michigan, during a fire-drill exercise.

Postwar America also saw some oddities emerge as the industry attempted to tackle innovative ways to fight flames. The Hahan Motor Co. attempted to introduce the Dual Spangler, named for the company's president, D. Herbert Spangler. This vehicle was powered by twin Ford V8 engines and carried a pair of 500-gpm [1,892.5l] front-mounted pumps, two 300-foot [91.4m] booster hose lines, and a 1,500-gallon [5,677.5l] water tank. Despite its huge size, it was designed to tackle rough terrain, but it failed miserably. Only the prototype was built, and after few years of service, it was dismantled for parts.

In 1948, Mack introduced an aerial ladder truck, the first new one since 1936. Maxim supplied metal aerials in lengths of 65, 75, and 85 feet [19.8, 22.9, and 25.9m].

Kenworth, long a proud name in commercial trucking, also produced a series of fire engines; Los Angeles was a frequent customer. In 1948, the city purchased a Kenworth Heavy Utility or "Heavy U" powered by a Hall-Scott engine

and equipped with a Holmes wrecker winch and an acetylene torch. The Los Angeles city and county fire departments are in the unusual position of having to service both highly developed urban areas and large patches of rugged wilderness. For this reason, heavy-duty wreckers such as the Kenworth are common pieces of equipment for both the county and city fire departments.

Commercial rigs were just as common in the Los Angeles area fire-fighting community as big custom jobs. In 1947, the U.S. Forestry Service sent a Ford cab-over-engine model, powered by a flathead V8 engine, to its San Bernardino, California, headquarters. The Ford was the popular Model 47 Tanker Marmon Herrington All Wheel Drive. It's now in the hands of Dan Gosnell of San Bernardino. And in 1948, a GMC powered by a six-cylinder 270-cubic-inch [1,650cc] engine was sent to the Department of Natural Resources, Division of Forestry, in southern California. It was equipped with a two-stage cen-

An open-cab 1948 American LaFrance 700 Series 750-gpm [2,838.8] pumper. Note the trio of searchlights at the midsection.

trifugal pump with a 400-gallon [1,514l] tank and a pumping capacity of 250 gpm [946.3l]. It now belongs to the Yucaipa Valley Fire and Rescue Association in California.

Meanwhile, a new name emerged as a fire engine maker. Crown Coach Corp. of Los Angeles hit the market with some fine examples of large pumpers. It constructed a custom-built 1,250-gpm [4,731.3l] pumper for the West Covina, California, fire department. Crown Coach saw its stock rise in the industry, and continued to build large and small apparatus for many California communities, using the Waterous pump and the Hall-Scott engine.

OVERSEAS

Postwar Europe was in shambles, and few municipalities could afford to order new equipment. As a consequence, 1930s-style fire engines remained in service for many years.

Dennis Brothers remained the leading maker of fire-fighting apparatus and offered a wide range of products. The company's first efforts after the war were to produce a new fire chassis with an open cab or truck cab that featured the traditional front hood and grille. Though Dennis had always built its own engines, it switched to the Rolls-Royce gasoline engine because of its advanced technology.

In addition to making some significant changes in their power unit and chassis, Dennis purchased the British franchise for the German Metz turntable-ladder, which was mounted on a forward-control chassis.

Merryweather, meanwhile, decided to abandon its Albion-Merryweather chassis for the lighter and better constructed Bedford and Commer chassis.

Other European builders of the era—some new to the industry—were Kerr, Foamite, Morris, Angus, Sun, Hampshire, Haydon, Whitson, Carmichael, Campion, Pyrene, Miles, and Arlington.

LEFT: This 1966 photograph shows a 1934 Dennis Brothers fire engine about to be driven from London to Paris and back in order to commemorate the 300th anniversary of the Great Fire of London.
FOLLOWING PAGE: A 1950 Dodge pumper. Dodge wasn't in the business of manufacturing fire engines, but many municipalities converted the durable vehicles into fire-fighting units.

CUSTOM RIGS

More than 200 makes of fire engines were manufactured during much of this century in response to fire departments' demands that equipment be tailored to their specific needs.

During the early years, commercial truck builders—Ford, Chevrolet, and General Motors—produced many of the trucks that served American fire departments. They would deliver the frame, wheels, power train, and cowl to a fire equipment outfitter, which then installed the pump, hose body, racks for ladders, lights, siren or bell, and a number of compartments for tools and smaller equipment. Many small communities entered the gasoline-powered engine age by purchasing vehicles in this manner.

The Sierra Madre, California, volunteer fire department purchased its first motorized fire engine in June 1921 when it acquired a Pierce-Arrow. The automobile was quickly remodeled—probably by the volunteers themselves—with a hose reel, hose racks, pump, and bell. It was named "Old Chief" and saw many years of service in the small foothill community.

The Howe Fire Apparatus Company, founded in 1872, often used commercial chassis as the basis for its line of fire engines. It usually built its equipment on Ford

A Howe Defender that for many years served the city of Roslyn, Washington.

Model A chassis. In the 1930s, it began marketing its Howe Defenders, which were constructed on Defiance truck chassis.

Each year, Chevrolet issued its Silver Book, which published advertisements from truck body builders and fire equipment suppliers. These books were sent to dealers and allowed municipalities to pick and choose what kind of equipment best suited their needs.

Although most departments purchased their vehicles this way, other more wealthy cities rewarded their volunteer firefighters by commissioning custom rigs.

These rigs were built from scratch to meet the buyer's specifications. They were the best-made fire engines anywhere in the world and had a price tag to match. Leading custom builders were Seagrave, Pirsch & Sons, Mack, Maxim, Stutz, American LaFrance, and Ahrens-Fox.

According to *American Volunteer Fire Trucks*, by Donald F. Wood and Wayne Sorensen, Ward LaFrance reported in the early 1970s that

> [c]ommercial trucks are less expensive than the custom type, but are limited in features. For the production of a commercial truck the manufacturer purchases the chassis, complete drive train, and cab from a major truck producer such as Ford, GMC, Dodge, or International. The pump is installed, and the tank and rear body sections are fabricated and mounted on the purchased chassis. A limited number of options are available as to the engine size, pump capacity and tank size.
>
> A custom vehicle is built completely to the customer's specifications. Such vehicles are normally more expensive than commercial vehicles and are usually more profitable to manufacture and sell.

One of the sexiest custom builders was Stutz, founded by Harry Stutz, who built marvelous racing cars and produced the Stutz Bearcat, whose name instantly evokes the Roaring Twenties and bathtub gin.

Stutz sold off his interests in his automotive company and founded a new automobile line called HCS. It failed miserably, but his other line of vehicles attracted wide attention in the 1920s.

Stutz began building fire engines in Indianapolis in 1919. His first was a triple combination pumper. The city of Indianapolis was so impressed that it purchased thirty-five fire engines from Stutz. In 1923, the maker offered a 1,200-gpm [4,542l] pumper. It also offered the Model K, a 350-gpm [1,324.8l] that was identified as the Baby Stutz.

This was the smallest offering in the Stutz line. One such rig was delivered to Havre de Grace, Maryland, in 1924. It served the city until 1935, when it was traded to the New Stutz Fire Engine Company, a successor to the original Stutz company. It was then sold to Farmland, Indiana, serving the town until 1950.

Custom rig manufacturers at one point numbered about eighteen, but that list has now dwindled to fewer than six.

ABOVE: The hood of a vintage Mack fire engine features the famous bulldog, instantly identifiable as a symbol of toughness and durability.
RIGHT TOP: The Ardmore, Pennsylvania, fire department purchased this rare Autocar high-pressure 70-gpm [265l] fog unit specifically to fight small fires with fog rather than water. An Autocar high-pressure fog unit can be seen at the Hall of Flame Museum in Phoenix, Arizona.
RIGHT BOTTOM: In the late 1940s, wooden ladders were arguably a fire department's most important pieces of rescue equipment.

A typical postwar offering by Dennis was the Dennis F1, which started the Dennis F Series. The F1 was a conventional pumper powered by a four-cylinder 70-horsepower gasoline engine with a rear-mounted, multistage turbine pump. The pump provided 400 gpm [1,514l].

The F1 was designed with only a 7-foot-wide [2.1m] chassis to navigate narrow country roads and villages with tight corners and high walls.

The F2 followed with the same theme and was powered by an eight-cylinder Rolls-Royce B80 engine. Perhaps Dennis's crowning achievement in the F range was the F7, introduced in 1949. It was a popular engine equipped with a mid-mounted 900-gpm [3,406.5l] pump that was exceedingly reliable and could go from zero to 60 mph [96kph] in forty-five seconds.

One of the leading manufacturers in airfield tenders was Pyrene, which mounted its bodies on Dodge and Bedford chassis. The Bedford QL model debuted in 1947 and was equipped with a 500-gallon [1,892.5l] water tank and 30 gallons [113.6l] of foam compound. It also featured a 75-horsepower Coventry Climax 400-gpm [1.514l] pumper

HIGH-PRESSURE FOG ENGINE

One of the more innovative technologies resulting from World War II was the high-pressure fog unit developed by the U.S. Navy.

Built to fight ship fires, these pumps could deliver a fog of water under extremely high pressure. The unit rapidly lowered high temperatures in ship compartments, preventing the blaze from sustaining itself. It also provided an atmosphere that allowed firefighters to breathe. It used little water and required just a small pump to operate. It also reduced water damage to structures.

Autocar produced a high-pressure fog engine in 1950 that could put water to flame less than fifteen seconds after arriving on the scene. There was no need to find a hydrant.

The Autocar unit came equipped with a 500-gallon [1.892.5l] water tank that supplied 70 gpm [265l] at 700 pounds per square inch (psi) of pressure. It also featured two high-pressure hoses that could be used simultaneously. The engine was ideal for small fires in rooms or small attics.

Autocar delivered one of its fog engines to the city of Ardmore in Pennsylvania. It made more than 8,000 runs during its twenty-seven years of service, proving its effectiveness time and time again.

THE FIFTIES

As the twentieth century approached its halfway mark, firefighters began a maturing process. Safety finally became a paramount concern, with closed-cab engines a common sight on American streets. Two-way radios between firefighters in the field and the alarm room or mobile command unit provided instant communication for the first time. The Snorkel—which lifted firefighters into the air in a "cherry picker"—made its debut in 1958 and caught on like wildfire.

Wooden aerial ladders went the way of the steamer and bucket brigade, and airfield tenders—a product of World War II fire fighting—became a necessity for every major airport.

Along with these upbeat turns in the industry, there were also a few failures. The Buffalo Fire Appliance Co., respected for its quality and independence, shut its doors for the last time in 1948. And the bruised and battered Ahrens-Fox underwent another transformation when it was

absorbed in 1952 by General Truck Sales, a distributor for General Motors trucks.

Only the hardy—Seagrave, Mack, American LaFrance, and Pirsch—would survive to make significant contributions to the industry. There were others, of course, but the big four were virtually untouchable.

Ahrens-Fox was lucky to be around in any form to celebrate its centennial in 1952. After forty years of producing the flashy piston pumpers that were its trademark, it delivered its last one, a Model HT-1000, to Tarrytown, New York, in May 1952.

The takeover by General Truck Sales was an effort to keep Ahrens-Fox afloat. Costs were reduced by putting 650-gpm [2,460.3l] pumpers on standard General Motors chassis. However, few fire engines were sold. Less than a year after building its last piston pumper, the company again found itself with a new owner, the C. D. Beck Co.

But Ahrens-Fox was doomed. C. D. Beck was purchased outright by Mack that same year, and Ahrens-Fox's stunning cab-forward models were redesignated as Mack's C Series. Ahrens-Fox, which had survived numerous changes of ownership for over twenty years, delivered its last fire engine in 1957.

However, the Ahrens-Fox Fire Engine Company did not die; it merely stopped making fire engines. In 1957, Curt Nepper purchased the entire company, and continued to provide replacement parts and technical support to owners of Ahrens-Fox equipment. In 1993, in failing health, Nepper sold the company to the Menke family, who continue to run the company. Of the 1,500 fire engines built by Ahrens-Fox, nearly half still exist, and a handful, amazingly, are still in service.

Mack continued to be a strong presence in the industry. In late 1953, it introduced its most successful model, the B Series. It was produced through 1966 and became one of the

BELOW: A Seagrave pumper serving New York City rushes to an alarm.
FOLLOWING PAGE: This REO Speedwagon, with its distinctively classy radiator grille, serves as a light truck for the Pittsburgh Fire Department. In the background is another REO, outfitted as a delivery van.

The BEST
IS THE
JUICY FRUIT
different
P.B.F.
200
LIGHT UNIT
SPEED—WAGON
REO

A 1945 GMC 500 Series. Like Dodge, GMC was not in the business of building fire engines. Many GMC trucks, however, were customized as fire appliances.

A 1947 Pirsch 1,250-gpm pumper powered by a Hall-Scott gasoline engine. This model belonged to the Culver City, California, fire department.

A 1948 Mack with booster pump delivered to the Boston Fire Department.

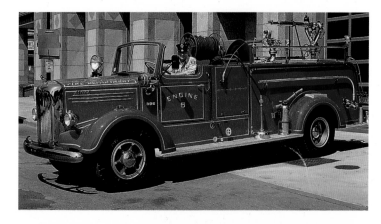

A 1941 closed-cab Seagrave 500-gpm [1,892.5l] pumper delivered to the Plymouth, Massachusetts, fire department. Trucks with 500-gpm [1,892.5l] pumping capacities were a perfect fit for small communities.

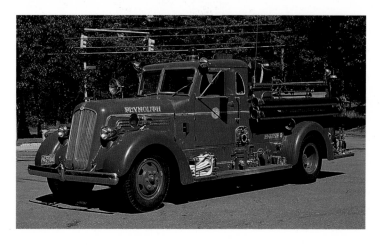

most common highway trucks in the United States and Canada. In all, more than 125,000 B Series models were manufactured.

Although highway truckers loved the B Series Mack, it was even more popular as a fire engine. It came as a pumper ranging from 500 to 1,250 gpm [1.892.5l to 4,731.3l], as a combination ladder truck, as a tanker, as a tractor-drawn aerial, and as a variety of other specialized apparatus. It had its trademark radiator with the Bulldog hood ornament, but the radiator was rounded at the front and nicely accentuated with massive streamlined front fenders. It was powered by the standard Mack Thermodyne overhead-valve six-cylinder engine.

The Model B-95, for example, could be equipped as a triple combination with an open semicab, two pairs of hard suction hoses on each side, and a hose reel located directly behind the cab. The Bureau of Fire in Chester, Pennsylvania, cherished its 75-foot [22.9m] aerial ladder truck, equipped with a set of red Roto-Ray lights mounted on a post near the windshield. And the city of Chicago ordered thirty Macks as combination pumpers and hose cars.

With the outbreak of the Korean War in 1950, the Cold War escalated. Fire fighting was married to civil defense planning as state and federal governments began funding training programs for both reserve firefighters and fallout shelter construction personnel in the event of a nuclear attack. Triangular "CD" emblems were placed on all fire appliances. For some time after the close of the war, CD emblems were still to be found on fire apparatus, and the legacy of civil defense lasted for many years as reserve training programs continued.

American LaFrance benefited directly from the war when it won a contract from the U.S. Air Force. Between 1950 and 1953, American LaFrance constructed more than 1,100 special crash trucks identified as Type 0-11 and 0-11A. These units, which were designed to travel over rough ground at high speeds and throw a stream of foam on the move, were sent to virtually every air force installation around the world. Many of these rugged rigs were still in service up until the late 1970s.

In 1954, Ward LaFrance offered a restyled Fireball Special Series. These smaller pumpers, with 500-gpm [1.892.5l] pumps, were designed for rural fire fighting and were powered by the Chrysler Fire Power V8 with a rated horsepower of 183. That same year, Ward LaFrance delivered twenty-five new civil defense pumpers to the New York City Fire Department.

American LaFrance also began offering smaller pumpers to attract smaller communities. These were, in effect, baby cab-forward Series 700s featuring a six-cylinder engine manufactured by Continental. The three small versions were identified as the 500-gpm [1.892.5l] Ranger, the 750-gpm [2,838.8l] Protector, and the 1,000-gpm [3,785l] Crusader. In addition, the company designed a new Twinflow centrifugal pump.

American LaFrance underwent two significant changes in 1956. First was its sale to the Serling Precision Corporation, although American LaFrance buyers saw hardly a ripple in services. Also during that year, the Series 700 was replaced with the Series 800. Aside from a minor face-lift and additional equipment compartments, there was hardly any change from the Series 700. But in 1958, the 800 was replaced with the 900, which featured a lightweight chassis, wider cab, wraparound windshield, and eight different engines to choose from.

Seagrave, meanwhile, competed fiercely with Mack and American LaFrance. In 1956, Seagrave acquired the Maxim Motor Co., although the two companies remained separate units. Seagrave continued to maintain healthy and profitable contracts with major cities.

The city of Los Angeles purchased thirteen new Seagrave triple combinations in 1955 and 1956. They were equipped with 1,250-gpm [4,731l] pumps, 400-gallon [1,514l] tanks, and five-speed transmissions. The 1955 models were powered by Seagrave engines, whereas the 1956 versions had Hall-Scott engines.

THE SNORKEL

Perhaps the most dramatic advance in fire fighting, aside from American LaFrance's cab-forward design, was Chicago fire commissioner Robert Quinn's Snorkel.

In 1958, Quinn was walking down a street in downtown Chicago when he noticed a two-man crew using a cherry picker to wash a business sign. He immediately recognized that the device was ideally suited to fire fighting because it could provide aerial mobility for the firefighter.

Firefighters use a snorkel to fight a construction-site fire in Kansas City, Missouri.

Quinn had the Chicago Fire Department purchase a single 50-foot [15.2m] boom and basket from the Pitman Manufacturing Co. of Grandview, Missouri. The city's department shop mounted the cherry picker on a GMC 354 truck chassis. It was a crude affair, equipped with a 2-inch [5cm] nozzle in the basket fed by a 1,200-gpm [4,542l] pump. The total cost of the unit was $14,000.

Dubbed "Quinn's Snorkel," it debuted in October 1958. A few weeks later, it saw service at a four-alarm lumberyard fire. But its true test came on December 1 at the Our Lady of Angels School fire, which claimed the lives of ninety-two children and three teachers.

Newspaper photographers captured the Snorkel in use, and photos were splashed across the front page of every major newspaper in the country. Inquiries poured in from dozens of fire departments. Two additional Snorkels, 65 and 75 feet [19.8 and 22.9m] tall, appeared in 1959 mounted on Ford truck chassis.

In 1959, the Snorkel again proved itself when it was used to rescue sixty survivors of an elevated train collision. Each passenger was brought down to safety in the Snorkel. The future and success of the Snorkel was secured.

MORE CAB-FORWARDS

Twelve years after American LaFrance debuted its cab-forward engine, Seagrave and Maxim finally jumped on the bandwagon.

Chicago Fire Commissioner Robert Quinn (in the white coat), inventor of the snorkel, supervises a 1974 alarm at the Darling & Co. stockyards in Chicago.

Seagrave recognized as early as 1955 that cab-forward design was the future of fire engines. In 1957, Seagrave engineers began to design their own cab-forward. In June 1959, the company's first cab-forward engine was delivered to Jackson, Tennessee, but further deliveries of the new design had to wait until September.

The company continued to offer its conventional style, which was introduced in 1951 as the 70th Anniversary Series and was produced through 1970. But sales of cab-forward designs jumped dramatically and quickly became the company's sales leader.

Maxim introduced its own version the same year, and designated it the Model F. It was a styling marvel with crisp, clean lines.

With all of its success with the cab-forward design, American LaFrance could still manage to lay an egg. In 1960, the company manufactured two turbine-powered fire engines. They featured Boeing 325-horsepower gas turbines. One came in the form of a 900 Series 100-foot [30.5m] tractor-drawn aerial ladder truck with a five-man canopy cab that was delivered to Seattle. Other than a huge rear-angled stainless-steel exhaust stack from the top of the engine compartment, the Series 900 looked identical to the traditional version.

But the turbines were noisy, lacked braking power, and were very slow from a dead stop. Three years later, the concept was abandoned in favor of the conventional gasoline-powered engines.

LEFT: This 1962 75-foot [22.9m] Seagrave "Eagle" served the Nashville Fire Department.
FOLLOWING PAGE: American LaFrance continued to capitalize on the success of its cab-forward models with this 1956 1,000-gpm [3,785l] 800 Series. This model served the Saint Louis Fire Department.

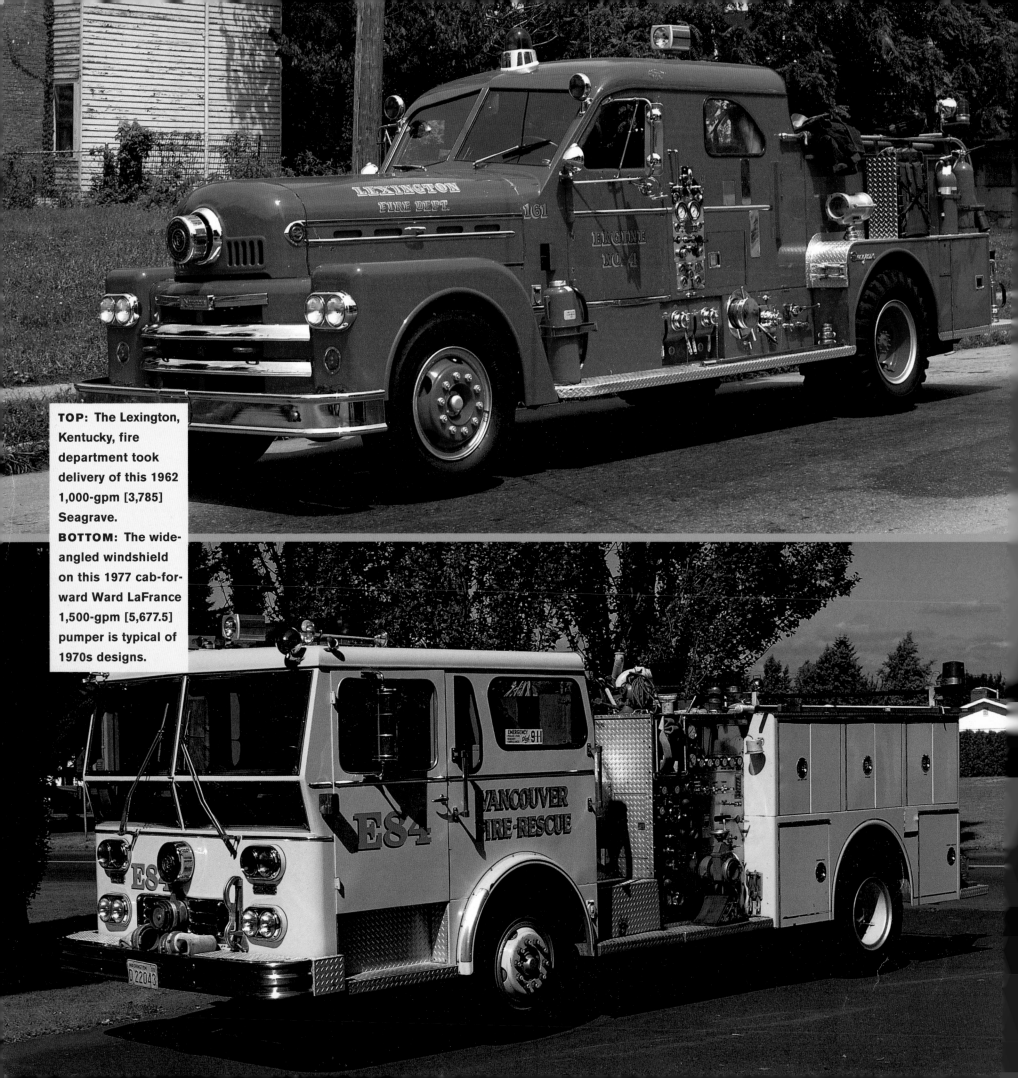

TOP: The Lexington, Kentucky, fire department took delivery of this 1962 1,000-gpm [3,785] Seagrave.

BOTTOM: The wide-angled windshield on this 1977 cab-forward Ward LaFrance 1,500-gpm [5,677.5] pumper is typical of 1970s designs.

CHAPTER FOUR

1961
1980

THINGS CHANGED RAPIDLY FOR THE FIRE-FIGHTING INDUSTRY DURING THE 1960s; THE MASSIVE SOCIAL UNREST THAT GRIPPED SOME CITIES CHANGED FOREVER HOW FIREFIGHTERS AP-PROACHED THEIR JOB.

Newark, New Jersey, firefighters battle flames shooting from several stores that were set ablaze during a 1967 race riot.
ABOVE: A uniformed National Guardsman takes up a position on a Crown fire engine during the 1965 Watts riots in Los Angeles.

The riots in Los Angeles in 1965 and in Detroit in 1967 illustrated for the first time that firefighters faced danger not only from fire but also sometimes from the very people they were attempting to save. The century-old image of the firefighter as a selfless hero crumbled in a few short years. Many people came instead to think of the firefighter as just another icon of government indifference to the working poor and oppressed minorities. Fire departments were perceived as all-white, all-male fraternities that had no place for other members of society. Fire departments, in short, were the Establishment.

The Watts riots in Los Angeles left thirty-four people dead, hundreds of buildings destroyed by fire, and $40 million in property damage; nearly 200 firefighters were injured. In Detroit forty-three people died, 1,300 buildings were destroyed, and $45 million worth of property was damaged. In both these incidents, fire departments were overwhelmed by the sheer number of simultaneous fires with which they had to contend.

In 1968, when riots erupted in the District of Columbia following the assassination of Martin Luther King, Jr., firefighters made use of lessons learned in Watts and Detroit. Fires erupted in numerous places, and firefighters developed strategies for "knocking down" fires. This meant isolating and reducing a fire to the point where it was no longer dangerous without taking the longer time needed to extinguish it fully. This allowed firefighters to move on to the next blaze that much sooner.

Still, these techniques did nothing to protect firefighters from the dangers inherent in a full-scale riot. During the Los Angeles riots of 1992, firefighters again were overwhelmed as hundreds of buildings burned. They not only faced the task of knocking down fires as quickly as possible, but they also found themselves performing their jobs under fire from gun-wielding rioters.

The civil rights movement of the 1960s did spark the slow-moving traditionalists of the fire-fighting community to implement affirmative action programs that allowed minorities into the fraternity (although the acceptance of women firefighters was still years away).

Another new trend of the time was that firefighters began to be trained more extensively in first aid. Administering first aid to fire victims had been a firefighter's job for a long time; in the 1960s, while fire safety continued to be their primary responsibility, firefighters expanded their duties to include more general emergency response. Emergency medical technicians joined fire squads and were

trained to treat anything from gunshot wounds and broken legs to heart attacks and seizures.

Meanwhile, fire engine makers reveled in the economic boom of the 1960s. Trucks sales were healthy, with more than 12 million registered trucks on the road in 1962. Chevrolet accounted for 4 million of those trucks, with Fords numbering more than 3 million. Mack, whose yearly production numbers were always relatively low, had 117,189 trucks on the road in 1962. Its best year was 1959, when it manufactured 12,709 new trucks, but by 1962 that figure had dropped to 5,780 new trucks. Those numbers may be deceptive, however, as Mack was responsible for

some of the most dramatic innovations in fire fighting during the decade, boosting its prestige in the industry.

The decade also witnessed technological advancements. The Snorkel had gained wide acceptance with fire departments across the country. By 1961, twenty-one Snorkels were in service at various departments. By 1967, that number would climb to more than 400. The aerial platforms were manufactured by a separate division of Pitman, the Snorkel Fire Equipment Co. of Grandview, Missouri. The Snorkel was usually mounted on a fire appliance or commercial truck chassis and could reach up to about 85 feet [25.9m].

A number of fire engine builders also began to offer their own aerial platforms. Seagrave, Mack, American LaFrance, and a smaller company, Sutphen Fire Equipment of Columbus, Ohio, all introduced aerial or elevating platforms between 1961 and 1966.

Seagrave was the first major manufacturer to develop its own aerial platform with its Seagrave-Cemco Eagle elevating platform that was offered at either 65 or 85 feet [19.8m or 25.9m]. This adaptable two-boom piece of equipment was built by Cemco and was designed to fit either a commercial truck chassis or Seagrave's cab-forward appliances. Although the majority of Seagrave's aerial platforms

The Butte, Montana, fire department took pride in its 1966 Mack C-85 75-foot [22.9m] aerial scope fire engine.

CANADIAN FIRE ENGINES

Today there is very little to distinguish Canadian fire-fighting techniques and equipment from those in the United States. Many of the leading U.S. suppliers of fire-fighting apparatus now have assembly plants in Canada or export equipment across the border. Indeed, Seagrave opened a plant in Windsor, Ontario, as early as 1903, and American-LaFrance established its assembly plant in Toronto in 1915.

Unsurprisingly, the emergence and development of Canadian equipment parallels the history of U.S. equipment quite closely. In the first decade of the twentieth century, just as in the United States, it seemed that just about every blacksmith's shop from Nova Scotia to British Columbia attempted at one time or another to establish an automotive manufacturing plant.

Many of these mom-and-pop operations quickly died out, but they helped bring Canada into the motorized age with a variety of hybrid fire engines.

Firefighters of the first two decades fought tooth and nail to keep their beloved horses, though municipal administrators quickly realized that motorized units were significantly less expensive to maintain. But in the western provinces, motorized apparatus was viewed with some skepticism, primarily because of the relative lack of paved roads and large areas of wilderness. As a result, some towns and even larger cities in the west used horse-drawn fire engines as late as 1938, while in the United States most horse-drawn units were retired by 1925.

Two successful Canadian manufacturers during those early years were Fotfredson and Gramm, both of which built sturdy chassis for fire engines. Nevertheless, even in those early years, most chassis were imported from the United States.

One of the most successful Canadian fire-equipment entrepreneurs was Robert Bickle. Bickle began supplying horse-drawn fire engines in the teens and 1920s in Winnipeg. He also built a very successful and popular hand pump for prairie fire fighting.

In the late 1920s, Bickle developed a relationship with Ahrens-Fox to sell pumpers in Canada. But Bickle soon discovered that the piston pump unique to Ahrens-Fox was too expensive for most of his potential customers, and he took delivery on only four Ahrens-Fox fire engines.

Later Bickle turned out his own fire engines, which were virtual copies of the old Ahrens-Fox machines. He constructed his own chassis and used a rotary-gear pump, powered by a Waukesha engine. His machines allowed him to compete in the customized fire engine market for many years.

Another prominent fire engine maker was Pierre Thibault, whose name continues to appear on Canadian firefighting equipment.

Thibault was a small-town French Canadian blacksmith who started building fire engines in Quebec in the 1920s. He made a fortune during World War II building hundreds of trailer pumps, and later switched to producing metal ladders.

While he built some apparatus and motorized units off of old Ford Model Ts, Thibault's success and name recognition in fire-fighting circles was based on his trailer pumps. In the hands of his nephews, however, Thibault's company went on to produce a wide range of modern pumpers.

One noticeable difference between Canadian and United States fire fighting is based on economic considerations. For a variety of reasons, Canadian fire departments in the early parts of the century had considerably less money to spend on equipment than did their U.S. counterparts, leading them to keep their older machines in service for far longer than in the United States. Even after World War II, when U.S. cities were clamoring for new trucks, especially cab-forward models, Canadian firefighters saw no need to rush to new equipment. As late as the 1960s, Canadian fire departments used an intriguing array of machines, and it was common to see very old and brand-new equipment fighting the same fires side by side.

In Duncan, British Columbia, firefighters rely on this Canadian-built 1982 Superior Ford fire engine.

LEFT: This 1987 Amertek Twin Agent Rapid Intervention Vehicle serves Vancouver International Airport.
BELOW: Thibault, one of Canada's most respected manufacturers of fire-fighting appliances, delivered this 1989 Spartan model to the town of Burnaby, British Columbia.

were limited to about 85 feet [25.9m], in 1961, it delivered a 100-foot [30.5m] version to the Excelsior Hook and Ladder Co. of Freeport, New York.

In 1963, Seagrave was sold to the FWD Corporation of Clintonville, Wisconsin, but the change of ownership did not affect its introduction of a new rear-mounted aerial dubbed the Seagrave Rear Admiral. Designed for the cab-forward models, the Rear Admiral aerial had its turntable mounted at the rear.

In the same year, Sutphen developed its own elevating platform, which featured a telescopic aluminum boom with a basket at the top. The first Sutphen effort was a 65-foot [19.8m] ladder mounted on a Ford C Series truck chassis.

American LaFrance came out with its platform in 1962. It was a 70-foot [21.3m] unit mounted on an open-cab Series 900 chassis. American LaFrance's version was unique in that its upper articulating boom unit rested into the lower boom

when not in use. Many of these platforms were fitted onto Series 900 chassis with completely enclosed rear bodies.

One year later the company debuted its new Aerio-Chief elevating platform that came in lengths of 70, 80, and 90 feet [21.3m, 24.4m, and 27.4m].

In the late 1960s, the Maxim Motor Company was equipping its cab-forward chassis with aerial platforms as well. Their Snorkels were Pitman elevating platforms mounted on chassis with tandem rear axles. A standard Maxim aerial usually featured a 1,250-gpm [4,731.3l] pump and an 85-foot [25.9m] Pitman. The unit was powered by a diesel engine, with bodywork by Pierce.

Maxim also introduced the Top-Trol, which allowed a firefighter at the top of the ladder to control the aerial ladder on his own, using an independent set of controls. The same controls were also provided for the firefighter at the aerial turntable console.

Mack was slow out of the gate with its elevating platform, but it finally introduced one in 1964, and dubbed it the Mack Aerialscope. It was 75 feet long [22.9m] and mounted on a standard C-Series custom cab-forward chassis. Like the Sutphen unit, the Mack version had a telescopic boom.

The Aerialscope consists of four rectangular-section metal tubes with the top three sections housed inside the lower section. It was mounted on a turntable base with a duplicate set of controls like that in the operator's cage.

The beauty of the Aerialscope was that it could be parked parallel to a structure and as far as 32 feet [9.8m] from its face. It allowed maximum coverage of the building, covering up to 6,850 square feet [2,087.9m] and ranging up to 65 feet [19.8m] above the ground. It was stabilized with four vertical hydraulic jacks at the corners of the vehicle and one on each side at the midpoint of the vehicle.

It was by far one of the most versatile pieces of equipment a fire department could own, serving as an observation platform, a lift for rescue work, or as a water tower.

Mack delivered a 65-foot [19.8m] Pitman Snorkel on a Mack cab-forward chassis with a completely closed rear end to the Glen Ellyn, Illinois, fire department. By 1966, several 100-foot [30.5m] aerials were delivered to the Chicago Fire Department.

In the 1970s, the Mack Aerialscope was commonplace among fire departments. The top of the line was a cab-forward engine with a tandem rear axle with interwheel and interaxle power divider, five-speed transmission, and powered by a 325-horsepower V8 Diesel engine.

During this period, Peter Pirsch & Sons used Mack chassis for their units. In 1964, a Mack C-Series canopy-cab tractor was used for its rig equipped with an 85-foot [25.9m] elevating platform. One rig was delivered to

Juneau, Alaska, took delivery on this 1963 American LaFrance 70-foot [20m] Aero-Chief, the first elevating-articulated platform built on a custom chassis by the company.

SLIME LIME

American firefighters derisively call it "slime green," the lime green color trotted out by Ward LaFrance in the early 1970s as an answer to safety concerns.

But there are some things that just can't be changed, even in the name of safety. And one of them is the traditional red color of a fire engine. Like a firefighter's mustache, it's an integral part of what fighting fires is all about.

Firefighters can stomach some colors besides red. White had been around since the advent of motorized apparatus. The city of Riverside took delivery of a pair of white Seagrave fire engines in 1909, and no one ever suggested that there was anything to be ashamed about in that.

But the debate rages on within fire department circles as to whether the color red should be abandoned for something more safety-minded.

Since the 1970s, ophthalmologists have argued that red is the worst color for an emergency fire vehicle, because it is not a color that can readily be seen at night. And no one really argues with that.

Dr. Peter Molloy, director of the Hall of Flame Museum in Phoenix, Arizona, won't nitpick over whether lime green is more visible at night than red. He'll even reluctantly concede the point. But with reflective stripes, pulsing strobe lights in red, blue, and orange, and sirens loud enough to wake the dead, he just doesn't think there's much point in trying to make a fire engine more visible.

"All those sirens and lights more than take care of any safety concerns," Molloy says.

The city of Santa Monica, California, ventured into the lime green, yellow, and even chartreuse color phenomenon in the 1970s, only to return to traditional red fifteen years later. One local joke was that people were mistaking the yellow engines for big taxis and flagging them down. The Oxnard, California, fire department went through the same thing. Both departments report that firefighter morale is up since the return to red.

Some fire department supervisors, with an eye to questions of liability, have a tendency to side with the ophthalmologists. Others, however, take the middle ground.

"Putting together all the visibility studies, I happen to belong to the traditionalists," said Bill Messersmith, a volunteer firefighter with the Sierra Madre, California, fire department. "But you can't put the studies totally aside. you have to pay attention and go with what you feel most comfortable with."

RIGHT: Most firefighters just can't get used to the yellow-green color of fire engines such as this ladder truck working for the Columbia, Missouri, fire department.
OPPOSITE: A Dalmatian settles in for guard duty in front of this American LaFrance unit at a firehouse on a U.S. Army post.

Kenosha, Wisconsin, featuring rear bodywork by Pirsch. Pirsch also developed a four-section, 100-foot [30.5m] aerial ladder on its tractor-drawn models. It was equipped with a fixed tillerman's seat.

In 1968, it supplied the Chicago Fire Department with a pair of rear-mounted 100-foot [30.5m] aerial ladders mounted on Mack Model CF cab-forward chassis. In 1971, an 85-foot [25.9m] version, also on a Mack Model CF chassis, was sent to Milwaukee.

THE AGE OF DIESEL

At the dawn of the decade, Mack had begun an intense campaign to persuade fire chiefs to switch from gasoline-powered engines to diesel. Mack's contention was that diesel was

cheaper and provided for more reliable engine performance in its apparatus. In July 1964, it offered stunning evidence that diesel was the fuel of the future for all fire apparatus.

Mack staged a test in Detroit to prove that its new Thermodyne diesel engines had the endurance necessary to battle huge fires. Using a 1,000-gpm [3,785l] Mack C-95 diesel pumper, the truck pumped water from the Detroit River for seven consecutive days without shutting down once. At the end of the test, fire chiefs discovered that the engine had pumped 10 million gallons [37.850,000l] of water, while consuming only 1,108 gallons [4,193.8l] of diesel fuel.

Mack had been toying with the idea of using diesel for several years. In 1960, Mack delivered three Mack B Model fire trucks powered by Thermodyne diesel engines to the city of Hamilton in Bermuda. Mack wasn't the first fire appara-

A firehouse Dalmatian surveys his kingdom from atop a unique Pierce/Ford 8000 "Custom Cab" pumper, which has thrown tradition to the wind with a bright lemon-yellow paint job rather than the traditional red.

tus maker to consider using diesel. The New Stutz Company installed a diesel engine on a fire engine in 1939. But Mack was the first to market the new fuel seriously.

By the end of 1962, Mack had found enough regular customers to make its diesel campaign a success. Two Pennsylvania cities and Cheyenne, Wyoming, each purchased a diesel-powered fire engine from Mack. By the late 1960s, Mack convinced enough fire departments that diesel was the future to make the new engine the power plant of choice for firefighters.

THE SUPER PUMPER

For more than a century, despite numerous technical innovations, firefighters had been faced with the fact that when battling truly huge blazes, they did not have the capability to deliver adequate amounts of water onto fires. Conventional pumps were still not powerful enough to jet streams of water onto flames at a long enough distance or in vast enough quantities. And if pumps had been sufficiently powerful, fire departments still lacked hoses that were strong enough to handle high pressure and large volumes of water.

Fireboats, at least, had unlimited supplies of water to draw from, but their success was limited strictly to waterfront areas.

The solutions to these problems eventually came from innovations developed by the U.S. and British navies. The U.S. Navy researched and produced a reliable high-pressure hose, while the British Admiralty introduced the Napier Deltic engine, a motor specifically manufactured for heavy-

Mack's Super Pumper System represented a huge improvement in fire-fighting capabilities. Here, the New York City Fire Department employs one element of the system, the Satellite 3.

duty work on boats. Mack realized that by coupling these two elements with a powerful pump, it could create fire apparatus dramatically more effective than anything previously built. In its most ambitious project yet, Mack developed what would be the most powerful land-based mobile fire-fighting vehicle complex ever.

Mack devised a system for major cities that included the Super Pumper, Super Tender, and Satellite Tender. It was designed to do the work of ten conventional pumpers. This complex was actually a mobile pumping station and portable pipeline. It could pump 8,800 gallons [33,308l] of water per minute at 350 psi through five huge hose lines.

The Napier Deltic engine was indeed impressive. It was a lightweight eighteen-cylinder diesel engine rated at 2,400 horsepower at 1,800 rpm. The cylinders were arranged in a triangle with two pistons per cylinder. It also featured three crankshafts geared together to drive a common output shaft. The engine was connected to a DeLaval six-stage centrifugal pump delivering 4,400 gpm [16,654l] at 700 psi or 8,800 gallons [33,308l] at 350 psi.

The Super Pumper was equipped with a massive rear winch to place its suction hose into a river or other large body of water. It could also draw water from as many as eight hydrants at one time. All told, Mack's Super Pumper could supply an unprecedented 37 tons [33.6t] of water per minute through thirty-five hose lines.

The Super Tender could generate 10,000 gpm [37,850l] from a water cannon mounted directly to the rear of the cab. The cannon could send a jet of water 600 feet [182.9m] high. It featured hydraulic outriggers to stabilize the vehicle while the cannon was in use. The Super Tender was also equipped with a five-axled articulated unit and with a tractor rig similar to the Super Pumper.

As many as three Satellite Tenders, which were each equipped with 2,000 feet [609.6m] of 4½-inch [11.4cm] hose, completed the Super Pumper complex. The Satellite Tenders had four-wheel drive, and each carried a 4,000 gpm [15,140l] water cannon. They generally arrived first at a fire scene to establish a position, to be linked up later with the Super Tender and Super Pumper.

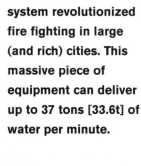

Mack's Super Pumper system revolutionized fire fighting in large (and rich) cities. This massive piece of equipment can deliver up to 37 tons [33.6t] of water per minute.

The first Super Pumper complex was delivered to New York City in 1965. The Chicago Fire Department purchased its Super Pumper in 1968.

THE END OF AN ERA

With the advent of the Super Pumper, diesel fuel, and aerial platforms that could reach dizzying heights, it's probably not surprising that the conventional fire engine—with its hood and engine in front—went the way of the horse and steamer.

Cab-forward engines were the rig of choice for most fire departments. Many departments still kept conventional rigs, but those were for auxiliary work rather than front-line action.

Seagrave stubbornly clung to the conventional look for many years. Although it did offer a cab-forward design, it continued to produce a conventional fire engine for its more traditional customers. Yet even those customers began to succumb to the cab-forward look. By the mid-1960s, Seagrave experienced a dramatic drop in sales of the conventional fire engine.

In 1965, Seagrave delivered its last three sedan pumpers to the Detroit Fire Department. They were 1,000-gpm [3,785l] sedans powered by Waukesha engines and constructed at Seagrave's new Clintonville, Wisconsin, plant under the new owners, FWD Corporation.

Another conventional sedan pumper to be built that year was the massive Seagrave rescue squad truck, using a Gerstenslager Corporation body featuring a front-mounted A-frame winch permanently attached to the chassis. The vehicle was tall enough in the rear to allow crew members to stand up. It was delivered to the Syracuse, New York, fire department.

CRASH TENDERS

World War II illustrated the necessity of developing an effective means to battling blazes at airports. Crash tenders, specialized fire engines for airports, are by far the biggest and costliest machines used to fight fires.

They are designed for fighting aircraft fires involving oil and aircraft fuel and for rescuing scores, if not hundreds, of passengers from blazing infernos of sheet metal. A 747 jumbo jet, for example, can carry nearly 500 passengers and thousands of gallons of fuel. A rig is needed not only to knock down a fire of catastrophic proportions but also to drive up next to the fuselage to conduct rescue operations.

Perhaps the most impressive vehicle of this kind is the FWD Aircraft Crash Tender manufactured by the FWD Corporation. Although this gigantic rig was specifically constructed for the U.S. Air Force, it is used by civilian departments with some modifications.

The four-wheel drive rig was placed on an eight-wheel chassis powered by twin 340-horsepower rear-mounted engines. It weighs a whopping 65,000 pounds [29,510kg], but can hit 55 mph [88kph] in less than sixty seconds, with a top speed of about 65 mph [104kph]. Its design allows it to hit high speeds over rough terrain. Its centrifugal pump allows the rig to deliver foam at 1,400-gpm [5,299l] from as far as 200 feet [61m] away less than two minutes after arriving on the scene. It also features a 2,300-gallon [8.705.5l] water tank and a 200-gallon [757l] foam compound tank.

Another popular crash truck is the Oshkosh T-3000, a 36-foot-long [11m], 12-foot-tall [3.6m] behemoth that sports a 3,000-gallon [11,355l] water tank and a 540-horsepower engine with a top speed of 65mph [104kph].

Several European manufacturers produced popular crash tenders. One such engine was the German-made Faun 8X8

ABOVE: Pump panels on a fire engine used by the Lewes, Delaware, fire company, Station 82.
LEFT TOP: In the early 1970s Ward LaFrance favored yellow over red for its appliances, such as this 1970 1,750-gpm [6,623.8l] pumper.
LEFT BOTTOM: A 1989 Oshkosh T-3000 is ready to roll at the Warwick, Rhode Island, airport.

Airfield Crash Tender. Specializing in eight-wheel vehicles since 1938, Faun produced foam and powder trucks. The tender is powered by a 1,000-horsepower Daimler-Benz V10 diesel engine with a four-speed power-shift transmission. It weighs about 53 tons [48.1t], and carries 19,026 gallons [72,013l] of water and 2,114 gallons [8,001l] of foam.

Faun's main competitor is the Kronenburg fire apparatus company, founded in 1823. In 1971, Kronenburg constructed a 4×4 Airfield Crash Tender and a 6×6 was introduced the following year.

The 4×4 is powered by a Daimler-Benz V8 turbocharged engine that produces 710 horsepower at 2,200 rpm. Weighing 30 tons [27.2t], it can reach 80 mph [128kph] in forty seconds. It carries 8,456 gallons [32,005l] of water and 1,057 gallons [4,000l] of foam, which can be pumped through a two-stage centrifugal pump powered by its own six-cylinder motor.

The 6×6 unit uses a pair of General Motors V8 diesel engines with a GM V6 to power a 2,000-gpm [7,570l] pump. It also features a 6,130-gallon [23,202l] water tank and a 1,268-gallon [4,799l] foam tank inside the body.

The British Bedford-Pyrene Airfield Crash Tender was placed on a wheelbase of 11 feet, 11 inches [3.5m] and had four-wheel drive. Powered by a six-cylinder engine with 72 braking horsepower at 3,000 rpm, it featured two 4-inch [20.2cm] canvas hoses 80 feet [24.4m] long. Foam compound was stored in a 40-gallon [151.4l] tank.

OTHER FOREIGN VEHICLES

Whether it was an airfield crash tender or a small four-wheel drive unit, vehicles capable of crossing rough terrain were vital to having a complete fire-fighting arsenal. In England, Australia, and New Zealand, there are rural areas where only four-wheel drive apparatus will serve to battle fires.

Many fire agencies filled this need with the Land-Rover, a sturdy vehicle manufactured by the Rover Company, a division of the British Leyland Motor Corporation.

OPPOSITE PAGE: By the 1970s, Seagrave had abandoned the conventional look entirely in favor of cab-forward models, a style typified by this fire engine. The Chicago Fire Department's Truck Company No. 7 is mopping up after a blaze on the north side.
LEFT: The Tennessee National Guard uses a U.S. Air Force American LaFrance fire unit in Memphis.

Land Rovers have long been a common sight on American and British roads, and they gained considerable fame as the most desirable truck to own in Australia. And it's no wonder. These lightweight vehicles are extremely mobile in tough terrain, can climb the toughest hills and mountainsides, and can ferry men and equipment about easily. All this is incorporated into a vehicle that is reasonably attractive and can double for civilian street use.

Popular versions of the Land-Rover were the Carmichael Redwing forward-control version and the HCB-Angus Firefly light fire appliance.

The Carmichael Redwing was mounted on a heavy-duty chassis and was completely enclosed as a van with side windows, numerous compartments for first-aid gear, and a ladder mounted on top.

The HCB-Angus Firefly offered similar features, but because it was dramatically smaller than the Redwing, the Firefly could cover rough ground in tight places. It resembled a utility pickup truck, with its compartments at the rear, a hose reel directly behind the cab, and a ladder mounted over the roof of the cab.

The Alvis Salamander 6×6 Airfield Crash Tender, a rather odd-looking duck with bodywork by either Pyrene or Foamite, was manufactured in Great Britain for the Royal Air Force. It was converted for civilian departments and gained fame for its amphibious capability. This van was used as a rescue unit and crash tender for the fire brigade at Rangoon Harbour, and another version was used as an airfield and amphibious rescue unit for the RAF on the island of Guam in the Pacific.

This is an early version of the American LaFrance 90-foot [27.4m] Aero Chief with a massive 1,000-gpm [3,785l] pumping capacity. It was manufactured in 1971.

The Salamander was powered by a Rolls-Royce B81 six-cylinder rear-mounted engine with a rated braking horsepower of 240. The entire vehicle weighs 12 tons [10.9t].

Thornycroft manufactured more than 5,000 Nubian 4×4 chassis during World War II for use in England and offered a variety of crash tenders and pumpers for heavy-duty work. The Nubian II dual pumper, the Nubian 6×6 Airfield Crash Tender, and the Pyrene Protector mounted on a Thornycroft chassis saw extensive service in the 1960s.

These vehicles were powered by either a six-cylinder diesel or four-cylinder gasoline engine built by Rolls-Royce and could cover the most difficult ground. Bodywork came from such coachbuilders as Pyrene, Sun, Airfoam, and Carmichael. The Nubians gained wide popularity among firefighters in Finland and Australia.

France's Berliet GBK 18 4×4 forest firefighter, constructed in 1971, rivaled both of the top British offerings, Thorncraft's Nubian and the Alvis Salamander, in both reliability and performance.

Designed to fight forest fires, the Berliet featured a six-cylinder engine with 150 horsepower at 3,500 rpm. It could hit a top speed of 53 miles per hour [86kph]. It was capable of moving 60 cubic meters of water per hour, and contained a 3,700-quart [3,500l] water tank that discharged its contents through a pair of hoses. The all-steel cab could fit three firefighters and had a bench seat that could hold four more men.

The rig contained suction hoses mounted on each side of the unit, hoses, axes, ropes, a hose reel mounted at the rear of the water tank, hydrant standpipes, portable extinguishers, and nozzles.

LEFT: Firefighters brave heat and smoke to set a stream of water on a blaze below.
FOLLOWING PAGE: A closed-cab, cab-forward 1965 American LaFrance quad combination fire engine.

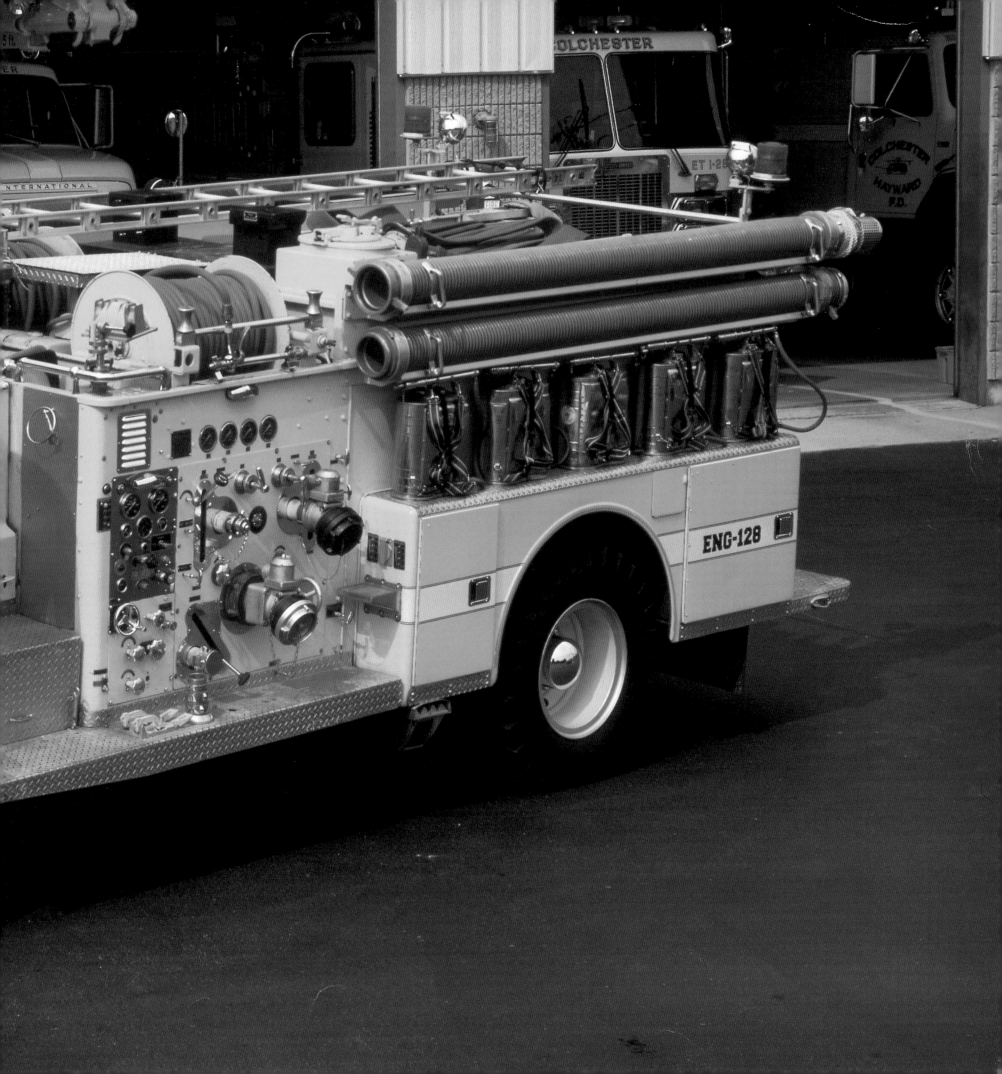

TOP: Big monsters like this 1985 Oshkosh T-12 often see service on U.S. military posts.
BOTTOM: The Bellevue, Washington, fire department took delivery on this 1994 Spartan 1,750-gpm [6,632.8l] pumper.

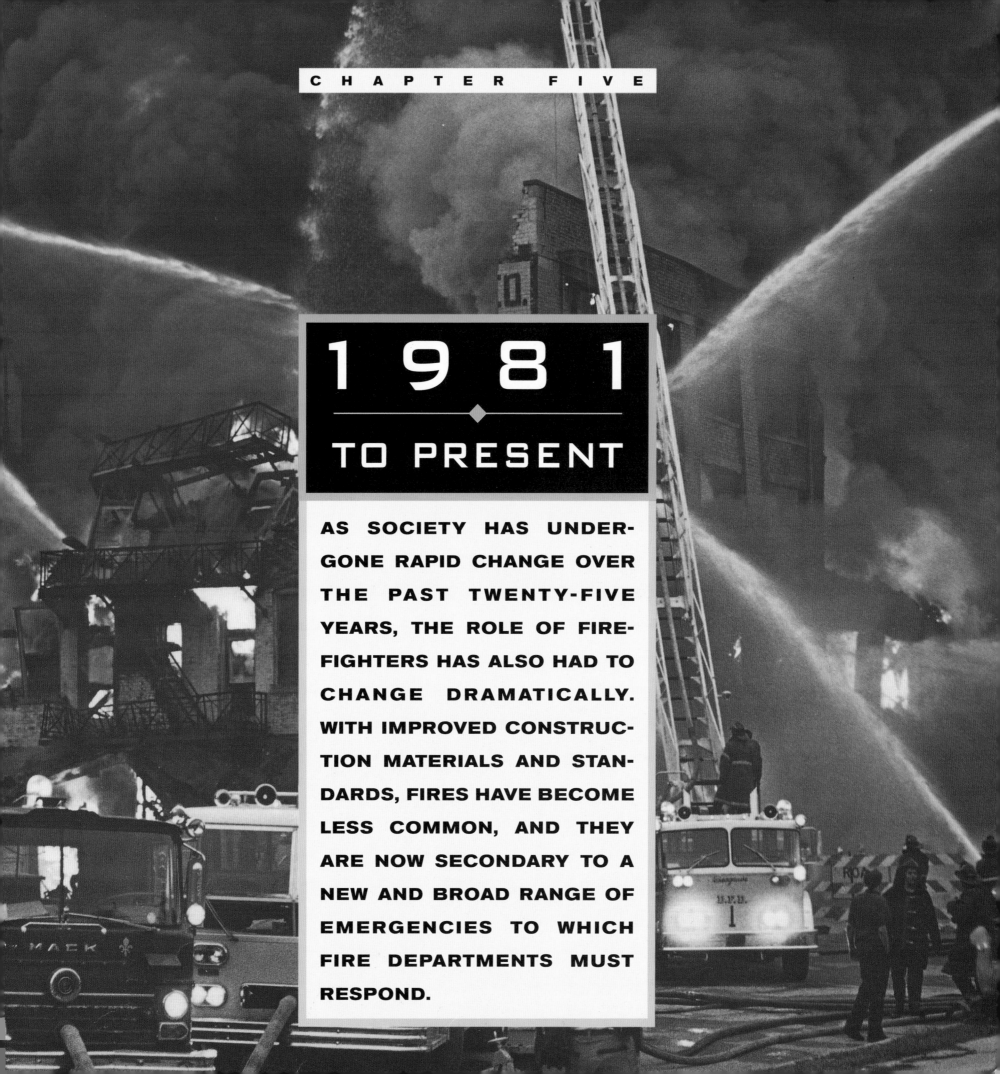

CHAPTER FIVE

1981
TO PRESENT

AS SOCIETY HAS UNDER-GONE RAPID CHANGE OVER THE PAST TWENTY-FIVE YEARS, THE ROLE OF FIRE-FIGHTERS HAS ALSO HAD TO CHANGE DRAMATICALLY. WITH IMPROVED CONSTRUC-TION MATERIALS AND STAN-DARDS, FIRES HAVE BECOME LESS COMMON, AND THEY ARE NOW SECONDARY TO A NEW AND BROAD RANGE OF EMERGENCIES TO WHICH FIRE DEPARTMENTS MUST RESPOND.

PREVIOUS PAGE:
The Detroit Fire
Department pulls out
all the stops in bat-
tling a five-alarm
blaze consuming two
warehouses near the
downtown area.

BELOW: Fire depart-
ments in the North-
west have been par-
ticularly fond of
Spartan fire engines.
This Spartan 1,500-
gpm [5,677.5l] pumper
belongs to the Seattle
Fire Department.

There will always be fire fighting, but since the 1970s, there has been a continuing shift in priorities. Firefighters now respond to more medical emergencies than blazes. And with the passage of hundreds of laws to protect the environment, the responsibility to identify and contain hazardous materials has fallen on fire departments.

Fire engines and equipment have become bigger, more complicated, and more specialized. Seagrave, Mack, Ward LaFrance, and other fire engine makers have been shifted from center stage, while younger manufacturers have now begun to offer the lion's share of state-of-the-art engines to fire departments. KME/Freightliner, Crown, Emergency-One or E-One, Spartan/Hi-Tech, and Simon/LTI are the names most often to be found on the fire engines in American fire departments these days.

The fire department in Riverside County, California, took delivery of seventeen Emergency-One triple combination pumpers in 1995. Each unit features a 1,500-gpm [5,677.5l] pump and a 500-gallon [1.892.5l] tank.

The Ontario, California, fire department purchased, also in 1995, three KME Medic-Engine 133 models with a 1,750-gpm [6,623.8l] pumping capability.

With these new makers on the scene, it was inevitable that names hitherto synonymous with fire engines would take a backseat or even die out. Two such names were Mack, which now limits its offerings in fire engines, and Peter Pirsch & Sons, which delivered its last pumper in 1991.

In 1978, Mack replaced its MB model, 18,000 of which had been produced since its introduction in 1963, with the MC/MR series. This series featured a low tilt-cab truck that offered better visibility and handling than the previous models. They were built as aerial ladders, tankers, tractors, and pumpers. The MB and MC/MR series chassis also allowed the construction of fully enclosed crew cabs and elaborate canopies.

In 1990, Mack announced that it would discontinue production of the CF, MC, and R Series custom fire chassis because it could not meet the new 1991 engine certification requirements. The cost of retooling to put Mack's new E-7

engine into these chassis was also too expensive. This put an end to custom chassis building by Mack, but it still offered other fire apparatus.

The California Department of Forestry and Fire Protection took delivery in 1995 of a Mack Series 300 cab and chassis brushfire engine that came equipped with a 220-horsepower diesel engine and an Allison transmission. It featured a 500-gpm [1.892.5l] pump and 650-gallon [2,460.3l] tank and could handle Class A foam operations.

Pirsch & Sons was not as lucky as Mack. The oldest manufacturing firm in Kenosha, Wisconsin, ceased operations on September 11, 1986, after 129 years of producing fire-fighting equipment.

Hass/Blondek, Inc. purchased the company for $1.6 million on February 9, 1987. Limited production began under the name of Peter Pirsch Company, but two years later, the company was forced into bankruptcy.

The company's inventory and property sat idle for nearly two years, until the limited partnership of D & J Ltd. bought it in April 1991. A month later, Kerry Poltrock, president of North Central Fire Apparatus Company, acquired the office building, ladder shop, and parking lot. He sold off Pirsch's remaining assets and ordered that its final pumper—unfinished and still in the plant—be completed and sold off.

Sold as a Pirsch product, this last pumper was delivered to the Osceola, Arkansas, fire department. It features a 350-horsepower diesel engine with an Allison 740D Heavy-Duty automatic transmission, two-stage 1,500-gpm [5,677.5l] pump, and 750-gallon [2,838.8l] tank. It has a five-man cab and is painted traditional red with white trim. Gold leaf trim and lettering was added by ex-Pirsch employee Terry Davis.

Like fire engine makers, municipalities were under very tight budgets for many years as revenue dwindled. Fire departments are no longer loyal to a single maker. A station full of Mack or Ward LaFrance fire engines is rare. Now fire engines are chosen solely on the basis of capability and price. Other vehicles such as Haz-mat response units or rescue squads now compete for the same dollars as ladder trucks and pumpers.

HAZ-MAT

Haz-mat ("hazardous materials") responses have become a full-time operation in virtually every major fire department. Alarms from gasoline spills to police drug lab seizures require Haz-mat expertise, either by radio communications or at the scene. In the process, firefighters are frequently exposed to a wide variety of toxins.

According to San Jacinto, California, firefighter Jim Avina, there are five different ways personnel are exposed to toxins: (1) responding to a hazardous materials spill where chemicals can be inhaled, ingested, absorbed, or even injected; (2) exposure to toxic products from combustion at structure fires, vehicles fires, or vegetation fires; (3) exposure to chemicals from an illegal drug lab; (4) exposure to communicable diseases during medical emergencies; and (5) exposure to exhaust fumes, cleaning supplies, pesticides, and herbicides.

A firefighter must first determine the level of protection needed to deal with a Haz-mat situation. Under Environmental Protection Agency guidelines, the use of protective clothing ranges from Level A—which demands the most protection—to Level D.

The following are the required clothing and equipment needed to protect a firefighter under specific levels:

Level A—Positive-pressure full-face-piece self-contained breathing apparatus (SCBA); positive-pressure, supplied-air respirator with escape for a full five-minute minimum

ABOVE: Exhausted firefighters watch helplessly as a blaze consumes an apartment building during the 1992 Los Angeles riots.
TOP LEFT: This 1983 Mack fire engine exemplifies modern design, with its massive windshield for great visibility and a roomy but functional cab. This model is a 1,500-gpm [5,677.5l] pumper.
BOTTOM LEFT: An updated version of the 1983 model is this 1994 Mack MS-Master 300 Series serving the California Department of Forestry.

WOMEN FIREFIGHTERS

Despite the lure of earning a good living in an exciting and rewarding job, the number of women firefighters in U.S. fire departments remains pitifully low.

Arlington County, Virginia, earned the distinction of hiring the country's first woman firefighter in 1974, but the move hardly constituted a breakthrough for women nationwide. Only 4,000 women have put on the uniform since then, accounting for less than 2 percent of the country's 250,000 paid firefighters.

Fire fighting today can be a very lucrative job. Los Angeles County, for example, pays an average of $35,000 a year to a firefighter for working ten twenty-four hour shifts each month. Veteran firefighters earning promotions and overtime can take in as much as $100,000 per year.

Upper body strength is a major hurdle any female applicant must overcome. In addition to carrying 40 pounds [18.2kg] of heavy clothing and equipment on their backs, fire fighters must drag heavy hoses and lift ladders that sometimes require as many as six strong men to carry. During a recent training program for Los Angeles County, more than half the male applicants passed the physical entrance test, while only six of the thirty-six female applicants passed.

In 1994, New York City hired its first woman in twelve years. Its failure rate for women is incredibly high, primarily because of a ranking system that puts an emphasis on how fast a candidate completes strenuous training events. In virtually every category, the male applicant wins handily.

As a result, the percentages of women in most major fire departments are dismally low. Less than 1 percent of Los Angeles County's 2,400 firefighters are women. Los Angeles City Fire Department fares little better, with 2 percent women. San Francisco's department does somewhat better, with 5 percent women.

The leader in the fire industry, however, is the city of San Diego, with 8.4 percent of its 836 fire fighters being women. The city attempted to break the male fraternity in 1974 by hiring five female recruits, only to see them wash out. Four years later, two women were hired, but they had to pay a price familiar to many women who have been the first to break into male-dominated professions. They faced harassment and hazing and were placed under tremendous pressure—both by men hoping they'd fail and women demanding that they succeed.

But since the 1980s, with the help of the local firefighting union in San Diego, harassment and hazing has dropped dramatically. The San Diego Fire Department has since adopted policies regarding pregnancy and maternity leave. Any firefighter who becomes pregnant is entitled to a transfer to a non-hazardous job.

The city has become a role model for other departments. It recently became the first department to have an all-female engine company, consisting of a captain, an engineer, and two firefighters.

Although San Diego makes steady progress in the field, the obstacles women face in other departments can be very difficult to overcome. A federal judge recently ruled that it was a violation of free speech and press to ban *Playboy* magazine, which many women find offensive, from Los Angeles County Fire Department stations. Los Angeles City Fire Department came under fire after it was leaked that fire department brass kept a collection of videos of women applicants failing difficult physical endurance tests, dubbed "female follies." And in San Francisco, the fire department has been embroiled in litigation over alleged discrimination.

While there is still a long way to go toward making hiring practices of firefighters equitable, cities such as San Diego are quickly setting the standard for other departments to follow.

In July 1995, the Los Angeles Fire Department began considering sweeping changes to eliminate sexual and racial harassment of firefighters.

A report filed by a special committee came on the heels of an audit that determined that white men monopolized the fire department's top posts. It recommended the fire department establish a human relations unit to investigate complaints, hire a full-time sexual harassment counselor and full-time affirmative action coordinator, and provide diversity training programs.

The report is one of several moves by the fire department to open its ranks to women and minorities.

duration; totally encapsulating chemical protective suit; outer and inner chemical-resistant gloves; chemical-resistant boots with steel toe and shank; and a two-way communications system.

Level B—SCBA full-face-piece and SCBA positive-pressure, supplied-air respirator; hooded chemical-resistant clothing; outer and inner chemical-resistant gloves; and chemical-resistant boots with steel toe and shank.

Level C—Full-face-piece or half mask air-purifying respirators; hooded chemical-resistant clothing; outer and inner chemical-resistant gloves; and chemical-resistant boots with steel toe and shank.

Level D—No respiratory protection is required. Coveralls may be used as protective clothing with chemical-resistant boots with steel toe and shank.

There are many different types of boots firefighters can use to protect themselves, depending on the chemicals. The same applies to gloves, although many departments are shifting to Silver Shield disposable gloves, which can be worn with inner and outer surgical-type gloves to allow dexterity.

Many departments have developed Haz-mat strategy to include elaborate command units, particularly in urban areas. The city of Riverside, for example, received a grant to purchase its own Hazardous Materials Response Unit.

This massive motor home features a body by coachbuilder Fleetwood of Riverside, California. It's fully equipped with state-of-the-art equipment and is one of three motor units for a seven-man crew. The unit includes a "first-responder" truck, which arrives first on the scene; an auxiliary truck to provide additional air tanks; and the mobile office/command center.

The center comes equipped with a television and video cassette recorder to allow personnel to videotape the scene to monitor wind direction and other elements that may affect a chemical hazard. The television also allows firefighters to observe news reports that may provide developments unknown to them in the event of a major incident. Riverside's unit is also equipped with a four-band radio.

Perhaps the most vital piece of equipment is the computer system that allows personnel to enter data acquired on the scene to identify a chemical. Using a Cameo code-breaking program, the computer can provide the general structure and properties of a chemical instantly. It also grades the fire and health hazard and provides advice on how best to achieve containment: what first aid to use, and what protective clothing is necessary.

The mobile unit is also equipped with a fax machine for direct communication with chemical companies, and testing

equipment that can immediately identify a toxin. Several pieces of handheld equipment can identify as many as 300 different gases and vapors.

Many departments have combined resources with other agencies to develop elite Haz-mat units to respond to major disasters. This new philosophy not only saves money but quickens response times to alarms, because departments no longer have to make formal requests for mutual aid.

In June 1995, Ventura County in California developed a plan to pool the resources of its various fire departments to train and equip crews to handle toxic spills. Uniting the Seabee base at Port Hueneme and the cities of Point Magu, Ventura, and Oxnard, the plan allows two Haz-mat crews from the closest agencies to the alarm to respond automatically. The plan also allows the Ventura County Fire Department to eliminate one of its nine-member crews because the slack is picked up by a cooperating fire agency. Any spill in the county is covered by the newly formed Haz-mat crew. No jobs are lost, as the crew dropped from the team is assigned to other duties.

THE FIREFIGHTER OF THE 90s

In addition to chemical hazards, the modern urban firefighter has another terrible danger to confront. Following the 1992 Los Angeles riots, firefighters across the country became concerned about a new threat to their safety—the sniper.

Firefighters during the riots found themselves dodging bullets. As a result, some agencies are funding bulletproof vests for their fire personnel.

In July 1995, the city of Santa Ana, California, authorized the purchase of 130 bulletproof vests at $400 each for its fire department personnel. It is also developing a formal policy requiring each firefighter to wear the vest in dangerous situations. The vests are especially important for firefighters working as paramedics, because they often respond to calls involving gunshot victims, finding themselves in volatile situations where the shooter may still be nearby.

Santa Ana is not alone. Its neighbors—the Orange County Fire Authority and the cities of Fountain Valley, Newport Beach, Anaheim, Orange, and Huntington Beach—also have requirements for their personnel to wear bulletproof vests. In addition to the financial cost of the vests, there is a toll to pay in the performance of firefighters who have to wear them. The 5-pound [2.3kg] vests add considerable weight to a firefighter already carrying about 40 pounds [18.2kg] of equipment. The vests become heavier when wet.

But this grim development is just a small part of the firefighter's job. Overall, fire-fighting techniques haven't changed all that much when it comes to knocking down structure fires or battling flames in the brush. And although firefighters may lament the passing of the traditional firefighter's image, there are very few who would give up the job.

OPPOSITE: Chicago firefighters use their aerial to climb into the blazing third floor of a building on the west side.
BELOW: In the face of rapid growth over the past twenty years, Mesa, Arizona, needed appliances that could handle taller structures. City officials found their answer in this 1987 E-One Hurricane 1,500-gpm [5,677.5l] pumper with a 95-foot [28.9m] tower.

GLOSSARY

Aerial: A fire ladder mounted on a turntable on top of the fire truck and extending up to one hundred feet [30.4m]. It was invented in the nineteenth century.

Ahrens-Fox Fire Engine Company: Founded by Chris Ahrens with his sons-in-law George Krapp and Charles Fox in 1908, the company was considered the top-of-the-line producer of fire engines. It is best known for its piston pumper mounted directly in front of the radiator.

American LaFrance: A leading producer of pumpers and aerial ladder trucks. It was founded in 1903.

Amoskeag: A New Hampshire firm manufacturing steam fire engines.

Apparatus: A term applied to any fire-fighting vehicle.

Appliance: A term applied to any fire-fighting vehicle.

Back out: Firefighter slang for retreating to a safer place.

Blow-up: A flare-up or the sudden increase of speed or intensity of a blaze.

Braidwood body: A fire engine body that has a fire-fighting crew facing outward on either side of the vehicle.

Buggy: Any fire department vehicle.

Cab-forward: A style of truck design pioneered by American LaFrance, with the cab located directly in front of the engine.

Cab-over-engine: A truck with its cab located directly over the engine.

Centrifugal pump: A revolving pump in which water is drawn to the center of the pump then expelled at the periphery.

Charged line: A hose with water running through it.

Chemical engine: A rig that uses carbon dioxide to expel water from a container under pressure.

Closed cab: Popularized by Mack in 1935, closed-cab fire engines were fully enclosed, sedan-type cabs designed to transport a fire-fighting crew to an alarm in safety.

Combination appliance: A fire engine with at least two functions. Most contain a main pump and ancillary tender, and also come in triple and quadruple combinations. A quadruple (or quad) combination is equipped with a pump, hose, booster tank, and ground ladder.

Conflagration: A very destructive fire, a fire storm, or a rapidly moving blaze. Putting water to flame usually is not enough to stop a conflagration.

Dennis Brothers: Founded initially as a bicycle manufacturing company in the 1890s, it sold its first fire engine in 1908 to the Bradford Fire Brigade in England.

Double-acting pump: A reciprocating pump with a single cylinder, in which the piston forces water out with an up-and-down stroke.

Double-decker: A manual pump that has two rows of firefighters on either side, with one row standing on the ground and the other on the pump.

End-pumper: A manual pump with handles at each end.

Escape: A ladder that reaches upper windows and roofs of buildings to help victims or firefighters escape. Ladder escapes may be mounted on the ground or on an appliance.

Faun: A German manufacturer of fire equipment founded in the nineteenth century, known for its Faun 8×8 airfield crash tender.

Firebrand: Any burning material that could start a fire.

Fire engine: A mobile mechanism that is designed to pump water onto a fire.

Fire line: Perimeter of a fire area within which only firefighters are allowed.

Fire storm: A violent, intense, or towering blaze, which sometimes appears tornadolike. It is unpredictable and can consume entire city blocks very quickly.

Fire truck: A truck that usually carries ladders or other fire equipment. A fire truck, unlike a fire engine, is not equipped with pumps.

Fly ladder: An extension ladder that is mounted at the top of the main ladder.

Foam tender: An appliance that uses foam to douse oil fires, usually at airports or factories.

Fuel: Combustible material.

General alarm: A very large fire. All available personnel are expected to respond.

GPM: Gallons per minute.

Haz-mat: Short for Hazardous Materials. A fire-fighting unit assigned specifically to identify and contain hazardous materials.

High-pressure hydrant: A hydrant with 160 to 300 pounds per square inch of water pressure.

Hook and ladder: An exclusively American appliance that is equipped with long ladders and hooks.

Hose tender: A small appliance that provides additional hose in varying lengths for major fires.

Jaws of Life: A cutting machine used usually to remove trapped motorists from crushed vehicles. It also contains a hydraulic pump powered by a gasoline engine to move heavy objects.

Knock down: A term used by firefighters, meaning to control and extinguish a fire.

LaFrance: Founded by Truckson Slocum LaFrance in Elmira, New York, the company joined the American Fire Engine Company in 1903 to become American LaFrance.

Ladder pipe: A nozzle mounted at the top of a manned aerial ladder to direct a single, strong stream of water onto a blaze.

Leyland: An early British manufacturer, which produced steam engines before delivering its first petrol engine to the Dublin Fire Brigade in 1910.

Low-pressure hydrant: A small hydrant with 40 to 60 pounds per square inch of water pressure.

Mack: A very successful truck and fire engine builder founded in 1900 in Brooklyn. It is popular for its Bulldog Model AC series, and was one of the first creators of the closed-cab fire engine.

Magirus: A longtime German manufacturer which had great success with its turntable ladders.

Manual: A hand-operated pump.

Maxim: One of the few smaller independent builders of fire engines to enjoy a long life before being absorbed by Seagrave in the mid-1950s. It was founded in 1914.

Merryweather: Leader of the English fire engine manufacturing firms. Founded by James Compton Merryweather in 1836. The company produced beautiful steamers, and delivered its first self-propelled steamer in 1899.

Oshkosh: An eight-wheeled fire apparatus used exclusively to fight aircraft fires. It carries 1,000 gallons [3,785l] of water and foam.

Piano-style: A pump designed in the shape of a piano.

Pirsch & Sons: This company perfected the hook-and-ladder wagon. It was founded in 1900 by Peter Pirsch in Kenosha, Wisconsin.

Piston pump: Popularized by Ahrens-Fox, the piston pump was powerful and reliable, but it was expensive and required considerable maintenance.

PSI: A measure of pressure, this stands for "pounds per square inch."

Reciprocating pump: A basic manual pump that works in a to-and-fro motion.

Rotary pump: A pump with interlocking, toothed wheels that provides a steady flow of water.

RPM: Revolutions per minute.

Seagrave: Maker of some of the most gracefully designed fire engines in the world. The company was founded in Detroit and later moved to Columbus, Ohio, where it developed chemical engines, pumpers, and aerial ladders. Its closed cab, or safety cab, was the most desirable of any closed-cab fire engine design.

Shand Mason: A stiff competitor to Merryweather, it was founded in 1851. It constructed and delivered its first steam engine in 1858.

Silsby: A leading builder of steam engines from Elmira, New York.

Slime lime: Derisive term used by some firefighters for the green-yellow color of some fire engines.

Smoke showing: Firefighters see smoke at a site.

Snorkel: Invented by Chicago Fire Commissioner Bob Quinn, the Snorkel is a hydraulically elevated platform or cherry picker on a two- or three-hinged boom. Used to fight fires from an elevated position or rescue victims from tall buildings. Once known as "Quinn's Snorkel."

Squirrel tail: A suction hose that is wrapped around either the back or front of a fire rig. Usually found on Van Pelt fire engines.

Tillerman: The firefighter who steers the rear end of a long fire engine.

Turntable ladder: A ladder mounted on a turntable base.

Vollies: Slang for volunteer firefighters.

Ward LaFrance: Founded in 1918, and not to be confused with a separate company, American LaFrance. Ward LaFrance focused on ladder trucks and was the first builder to introduce lime green as a color for fire engines.

Waterous Engine Works: One of the first companies in the United States to build self-propelled fire engines. Its first self-propelled pumper debuted in 1907.

Water tower: A tower mounted on a moving fire engine or truck in which water is run to the top of the tower by a pump to hit the source of a fire in a tall building.

Working fire: A structure with flames showing on the exterior when firefighters arrive.

BIBLIOGRAPHY

Automobile News, 1968 Almanac Issue.

Buff, Shelia. *Fire Engines in North America*. London: The Wellfleet Press, 1991.

Burgess-Wise, David. *Fire Engines and Firefighting*. Norwalk, Conn.: Longmeadow Press, 1977.

Burks, John. *Working Fire: The San Francisco Fire Department*. Mill Valley, Calif.: Mill Valley Squarebooks, 1982.

Commercial Car Journal, April 1963.

Cottrell, William H., Jr. *The Book of Fire*. Missoula, Mont.: Mountain Press Publishing, 1989.

Goodenough, Simon. *The Fire Engine: An Illustrated History*. New York: Chartwell Books, 1978.

Halberstadt, Hans. *The American Fire Engine*. Osceola, Wisc.: Motorbooks International, 1993.

Inland Empire Firefighter's Gazette, Vol. 1, Nos. 1-11.

Klass, George. *Fire Apparatus: A Pictorial History of the Los Angeles Fire Department*. Los Angeles: John M. Ruccione, 1974.

The Los Angeles Times, September 13, 1993; February 10, 1994; June 14, 1994; August 2, 1994; May 28, 1995; June 5, 1995; July 7, 1995; July 12, 1995.

PHOTO CREDITS

The Richard M. Adelman Collection: 10 bottom, 15, 18, 20–21, 24–25, 28, 29 bottom, 30 bottom, 33 bottom, 35, 37, 38–39, 40–41, 44–45, 49 second from top, 51, 52 bottom right, 54–55, 56 both, 58–59, 62–63, 64, 74 top right, 78 top, 80, 80–81, 82–83, 90-91, 95, 96, 99, 104 top, 112; © Jeff Schielke: 49 top

© Archive Photos: 43, 76–77; Express Newspapers: 69; Welgos: 75

© Mike Boucher: 32, 45 bottom, 78 bottom, 84 top, 97 left top, 107 top left

The Corbis-Bettmann Archive: Endpapers, 11, 12, 13, 14 top and bottom right, 24 bottom, 31, 42, 50, 57, 60; Acme: 61; Detail, painting by Opper: 10 top; Topical Press: 16; Underwood & Underwood: 17

© Dembinsky Photo Associates: 98, 115

Envision: © Wanda LaRock: 67; © MacDonald: 66

© Mark Downey: 93

© William B. Folsom: 97 right, 113

© Bill Hattersley: 29 top, 30 top, 34, 45 top, 48, 58 bottom, 72–73, 78 second from top, 84 bottom, 86–87, 100–101, 104 bottom, 107 bottom left, 114

© Neal and Molly Jansen: 94

© Dan Lyons: 36

New England Stock Photography: © Fred M. Dole: 46–47, 70-71, 102–103, 110–111; © David A. Frye: 101; © Jean Higgins: 14 left, 23 top; © Clark Linehan: 6

© J.M. Mejuto: 19, 22, 33 right, 40 left, 52 bottom, 58 top, 74 bottom right

© Shaun P. Ryan: 49 second from bottom and bottom, 53, 68, 78 second from bottom, 97 left bottom

Tom Stack & Associates: © Bob Pool: 52 left

© Superstock: 24 left top

Underwood & Underwood: 27

Unicorn Stock Photos: © Royce L. Bair: 109; © Chris Boylan: 74 left; © Eric R. Berndt: 79; © David Cummings: 106; © Martha McBride: 92

UPI/Corbis-Bettmann: 65, 85, 86 left, 105; © Matt Mendolsohn: 107 right; © George Woodruff: 2

© Joel Woods: 23 bottom

© Terry Yip/Image Makers: 88, 89 both

INDEX